THE OFFICIAL NOVELIZATION

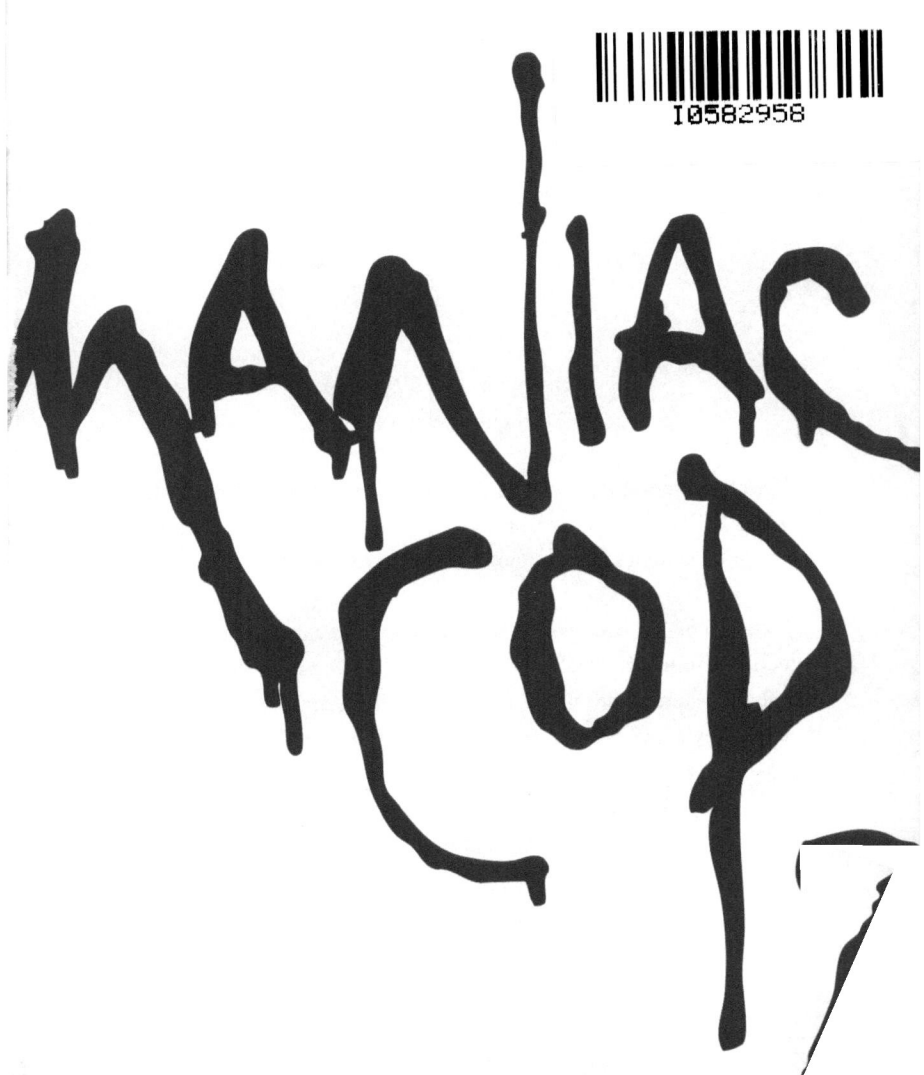

I0582958

CHRISTIAN FRANCIS
BASED ON THE SCREENPLAY BY LARRY COHEN

ISBN 978-1-916582-73-6 (paperback)
ISBN 978-1-916582-71-2 (ebook)

 ECHO ON PUBLISHING

visit: echohorror.com

Contents

Chapter 1

New York, December 1988

New York never forgets. It moves on because it has to, even though the scars remain. No matter the adversity, it picks itself up each time it is knocked down, brushes itself off, and carries on. It has always been that way. From Berkowitz terrorizing the summer of 1977 to the Brooklyn Theater fire that reduced hope to ashes, the city has always mourned its dead while learning to breathe again to face the next dawn.

For months after the dubbed Maniac Cop rampaged through its streets, the city had felt like it was holding its breath. Sure, New York had faced its share of monsters before, real and imagined, but this one had hit the city slightly differently. Maybe it was because he wore the uniform of trust, with the badge meant to symbolize protection and justice. Maybe it was because the killer didn't pick a type. There was no real pattern, no logic, not that any member of the public could see. He murdered anyone unlucky enough to cross his path.

The tabloids milked that fear for all it was worth, claiming sightings long after the events at Pier 14. "Maniac Cop Seen on Long Island!" screamed one headline, desperate to keep the story alive. Yet none of them whispered the name Matthew Cordell. They only knew the man's serial killer moniker, not the real identity of the impossible force. People spoke of the Maniac Cop in conspiratorial tones, saying he could have been many disgruntled police officers working in tandem or a serial killer playing dress-up to get closer to victims, but none of them spoke of the truth. None of them spoke of the tragedy and brutality that led to the mayhem that ravaged the St Patrick's Day parade.

Eventually, as it always had done before, life moved on in New York. The city forced itself to live to the next day. The subways were soon packed again, restaurants remained open late, and Times Square flashed its neon defiance twenty-four seven once more. But the scars were there for those who looked close enough. The places where he murdered were still avoided at night, with folks not quite ready to chance the impossible. They became no-go zones after dark, even for the hardened locals. The pier, where it all ended, stood like a corpse on the waterline, waiting for demolition. But because of what had happened, the developer had walked away from the project, unwilling to tempt any lingering bad luck that may still cling to it.

Eighteen months later, on a chilly September night, for most, it was a night like any other night. But across the East River in a vast auto graveyard of service vehicles, something was moving.

The lot, enclosed by high, razor-wire fences, was owned and managed by the city. Here, every police cruiser, fire engine, garbage truck, and ambulance met their ends. Some were riddled with bullet holes, others having been crushed from devastating collisions, but many were simply casualties of their time. Breaking down from their age or rendered obsolete by newer and more efficient models. No matter their reason, they were here, waiting to be disposed of.

Piled in high stacks, these forgotten, discarded vehicles created a maze of twisted metal across the expansive lot. To anyone who walked within it, navigating the crisscrossing paths, it felt like wandering through a city of scrapped metal skyscrapers as the stacks loomed high above them.

On this night, deep in this auto graveyard, past the bank of large compactors, a 1971 Plymouth Fury sat. Its two-tone black-and-white paint was faded and peeling as it bore the unmistakable markings of its former police life, complete with roof-mounted lights and a siren.

Someone was inside it. A large shadow.

Then a deep roar from this ex-police cruiser shattered the stillness around it. The Plymouth Fury's long-dormant engine growled to life. This sound reverberated around the stacks as the car's cracked headlamps soon flickered on, and its yellow beams shone brightly through the haze.

With no one around to bear witness, the car drove slowly through the stacks, toward the metal gate that hung limply from its hinges, having been wrenched open only an hour before. The old police cruiser having been resurrected after being long thought dead.

"What can I do for you?" the 7-Eleven clerk asked with a bored and disinterested tone.

Having clocked on at 6 p.m., he was seven hours into his night shift, and he hated every single minute of it. He despised having to speak to anyone who would come here in the dead of night. Because, in this part of town, it was always the same kind of clientele who ventured in. Junkies, bums, whores, hoods, and crooks —and this guy in front of him was, without a doubt, the former.

As the blinking sign outside stated, *Open 24 Hours: We Never Close*, this clerk wished it instead said, *Stink of Piss or Want to Steal? Don't Bother Coming In*.

The night shift hours were a slog as he watched the

dregs of the city's nocturnal life drift in and out. He felt stuck behind the counter in what he felt was a fluorescent-lit prison. Having to smile and nod, he pretended to care about the latest lowlife who wanted a pack of smokes, a lottery ticket, or whatever else they could afford with loose change that had been stolen, begged, or earned by illicit means.

He forced himself to look up, bracing for whatever request was about to come back from the customer. "Buddy? What do you want?" the clerk reworded after his first polite question went unanswered.

The gaunt-looking man in his thirties looked back with a glazed stare. His hair was long and greasy, his raincoat soiled with not just mud but all manner of fluids, bodily and other.

Great, the clerk thought. *This guy's either a shoplifter or even worse, someone wanting to talk to me or beg me for money.*

But the dirty man just smiled, a toothless, rotten grin born from years of crack and ignorance as his raincoat parted and the twin barrels of a sawn-off shotgun raised up and pointed directly at the clerk.

"What do I want?" the man slurred. "What d'ya think? Figure it the fuck out for yourself."

The clerk, though, was not scared or even surprised. He had been here many times before.

He just sighed loudly as he looked down to the same porno magazine he had been reading behind the counter all evening. "Listen, buddy," he said, not even meeting the man's crazed gaze, "everything we take goes down a slot into a safe in the basement. I don't know the safe combination, so can't help you with that. They won't tell me nor do they trust me with anything valuable. So, just do me a favor and fuck the fuck off."

He was more bored than scared, a script he had said many times since he started. This dirty man was not the first to think they could get the store's cash, nor would he be the last.

"I need money," the junkie grimaced, raising the gun up more threateningly.

The clerk shook his head. "Who doesn't?" he replied, still not looking up from the magazine, from the smile of the naked woman who stared back up at him. "Take some food and some booze, anything. The store's yours," he urged. "But as for money? I got nothin'."

The junkie was not impressed by this. His desperation seethed out of his mouth as he raised the shotgun to the ceiling. Pulling on the trigger, a shot rang out through the otherwise empty store and smashed the strip light above him. Sending shards of the tube downward and casting that part of the store into semi-darkness.

The clerk jolted at the sound but was still not scared. He just glared up from the magazine with a look of disdain.

With the shotgun leveled at the clerk once more as the junkie shouted. "You think I'm fuckin' with ya?"

He took a step nearer the counter and jabbed the gun forward. "That's gonna be you all over the fucking walls in a minute if you don't give me *all the goddamn money*."

The clerk looked at the gun, then at the junkie, then back down to his magazine. As he took a long breath in, his finger blindly reached under the countertop and pressed a red button. The store's silent alarm.

None the wiser, the junkie quickly and nervily looked around, making sure no one else was here or about to come in. From his twitching, profuse sweating, and constant chewing on his own cheek, this man was riding high on something, and he was coming down from it hard.

"Okay, I'll go through this again for you," the clerk said, his eyes rising to meet the junkie's stare. "The safe we have, I don't have access to. They don't trust me with access. So, there is literally zero way I can give you any money. No matter how much you threaten me with a gun, no matter even if you torture me, I can't possibly tell you something I don't know, can I?"

But the junkie's mind was not one that could fathom any logical argument or lateral thought. He just saw this clerk as a man standing in his way of being able to score more crack.

"You ain't listenin' to me," the junkie snarled. "I said give me the money, or I'll kill you."

The clerk shook his head, then looked back down

Christian Francis

at the magazine once more. He stared at the model's seductive expression and wondered what she would do if they'd swapped lives and he was parting his ass cheeks for this seedy publication while she was stuck in this hellhole.

Sitting at one of the many switchboards of the downtown police dispatch center, a uniformed officer leaned into the microphone. She read aloud from the latest report that flashed on her computer screen.

"Attention all units," she said clearly. "Possible two-eleven in progress, corner of 14th and 9th. 7-Eleven alarm activated. Officers approach with caution, possible armed suspects."

After a few moments of static, a voice replied, "Seven Adam eleven, this is car thirty-six, we're two minutes out."

"So, when does the boss come in?" the junkie persisted, jabbing the shotgun in the clerk's direction. "*They* can open the safe."

"He'd love that," the clerk replied, unable to hide his smirk while he kept his eyes downward. "He's in about six, six-thirty."

The junkie paused for a second as his brain swam in delusion and ill-formed thoughts. "Why don't I wait for him here, huh?" he said, nodding, as if he just had

8

the most genius thought. "You just go home. You don't have to be here. You could try running for the door, see if I decide to shoot you?"

"I'll stay," the clerk replied.

He may have hated his job, but the clerk knew full well that if he left, one of two things would happen. Either he would walk home and get fired for leaving the store unmanned, or he would get shot in the back as he walked away by this judgment-impaired addict. Both were unappealing options.

With a twitch of his eye, the junkie quickly smiled. "Well, how 'bout we have some fun then?" he pointed the shotgun to the lotto ticket display on the counter. "Why don't you open some up for me? See if I win anything? I feel lucky, you see?"

"Really?" The clerk could not hide his disdain. "From everything you've done tonight, you feel *lucky*?"

The junkie let out a sickly laugh as his eyes stared wildly. "Do it," he said, lifting the aim of the shotgun up to the clerk's head.

With another sigh, the clerk reached for a stack of lotto tickets. Slowly and without much care, he then, ticket by ticket, began tearing off their perforated edges. As each ticket was removed, the clerk scratched at their numbers. As each one was completed, in this unlit part of the convenience store, he had to squint at the numbers to check them.

"Nothing," he said as he cast the first ticket to one side and started on the next. "Nope."

"Keep going," the junkie urged, getting more agitated. "Better find me a winner."

"Sure," the clerk replied. "I'll get right on that."

"What d'ya wanna bet?" the cop asked as he zipped through the streets.

His belly was so large it almost choked the bottom of the steering wheel as he steered around the tight corners on his way to the call.

His partner, sitting in the passenger seat in the same uniform, sipped from a Styrofoam cup of cold coffee. "It's the 7-Eleven, right? Then we got three possibilities. Asshole tripped it by accident, wasting our time. Or they're getting stuck up, which'll also be a waste of our time 'cause of the amount of paperwork. Or . . . the alarm is bust—"

"Which is a waste of our time," the driver concluded.

"Exactly."

The radio crackled with static. "Car thirty-six, car thirty-six, be advised—car twenty-one is also en route to your location. ETA approximately five minutes. Acknowledge."

"They don't trust us to do this on our own, I guess," the passenger cop snickered, picking up the radio mic. "Dispatch. Car thirty-six. Copy that."

. . .

The clerk was over twenty lotto tickets into the junkie's demand. "Nope, this is a loser, too," he said, casting the scratched ticket to one side, then reaching for another.

The barrel of the shotgun was still aimed but moved even closer to the clerk's head, coming to a stop mere inches away.

"You callin' me a loser, huh?" the junkie said with a sneer.

His condition had shifted his emotions rapidly. From humor, to anger, to paranoia, to hate, then back again, he was not able to stick to one for long.

The clerk did not even look up as he continued to scratch off more lotto tickets. "These tickets so far, they're all losers. *Not* you."

The junkie suddenly flared with fury as he shouted, "How do I know you're not lying to me?"

The clerk paused for a second, realizing how unhinged this man truly was. Slowly, he put the card down on the counter and raised his hands in surrender, still staring downward, avoiding any eye contact. "Hey, I'm just callin' 'em as I see 'em. Nothing's coming up on the cards." He motioned to the small pile of discarded cards "You can look for yourself, see I'm not lyin', or just take them with you to make sure."

As the junkie looked down to the pile of cards, trying to see the numbers, he did not really understand any of it.

Then, a small shuffling noise at the back of the store caught the clerk's attention. Making sure the junkie didn't see him, he slyly peered up and had to force his lips to mask a sudden smile from crawling up his face.

Looking back down to the cards, diverging any attention away, the clerk then hurriedly picked one up. "Oh my god!" he said, with feigned excitement. "Look at *this* one! You were right!"

The junkie, confused, lowered the barrel slightly as he tried to look at the card in the clerk's hand. "What is it?"

"You won a grand! I'm not kiddin', a thousand bucks *right here*."

Suddenly lunging forward, the junkie ripped the lotto ticket out of the clerk's grip and looked at it. Before he could focus on the numbers, a louder noise from behind ripped his attention away.

Whirling, the junkies' eyes were met with a tall and powerful silhouette of a man dressed in a police uniform, standing in front of the freezer at the opposite end of the store. The uniform had no badge but was unmistakable as NYPD, complete with an eight-pointed hat, that hid the cop's face beneath a shadow.

"Fuck you, pig," the junkie said, not feeling any intimidation as he turned his weapon to the cop and immediately pulled the trigger.

The blast ripped through the aisle and caught the products on the left-hand side, the buckshot missing the target and, instead, finding a row of cereal packets that sent their sugary contents to the floor through torn cardboard and plastic.

The junkie frantically fumbled as he reloaded his weapon with the two loose shells from his filthy jacket pocket.

The cop, though, just stood in front of the refrigerators. Not reacting, not moving, as if waiting for the junkie's next move.

With his shotgun leveled again, the junkie closed one eye to aim the weapon. To try and ensure that his shot hit the intended target.

Firing, the shot rang down the aisle and into the glass of the freezer doors, smashing them on impact. As the glass sprayed out, a hazy, icy mist seeped out.

The cop remained still. Standing in the same place. He did not even flinch when the shot was fired. The shot where some of the cartridge's pellets would have hit him.

"I'll fucking end you," the junkie grumbled, upset that the cop was still standing as he aimed again and pulled the trigger.

Then, like a starting pistol, the bang of this third shot launched the cop into dashing down the aisle, striding toward the junkie aggressively. The clerk, seeing the approach, quickly ducked behind the counter.

With no shots in his weapon left, the junkie franticly searched his other pockets and luckily found the last two.

Even though he had managed to load these two shots into the weapon, it had made no difference. The cop moved fast, closing the gap between them in an instant. As he got close, he yanked a billy club from his belt and brought it down on the junkie's head with a vicious force, sending them to the floor before their gun could be aimed again.

With his head cracked open and dripping blood down his barely conscious face, the junkie struggled to focus or speak. The club hit so hard it stunned any and all thought from him.

"Thank god you showed up." The clerk smiled as he stood from behind the counter, seeing that the cop had subdued the gunman. "I was starting to think the alarm didn't work, and I'd have to put up with this asshole all night!"

The cop, without replying, reached down to the floor and picked up the junkie's fallen shotgun.

The clerk continued. "Can you believe it? That fucker thought he won a thousand bucks on a card. He actually believed me," he started to laugh. "I'm glad I distracted him enough for you. I guess all those plays in high school really paid off."

The smile on the clerk's face only had a second to drop before the shotgun was fired directly at him. The blast rang out as the pellets collided with his face, ripping into it with horrible ease. Decimating through the bone, brain, and muscle in a single pull of the trigger. As his body flew backward, a handful of lotto tickets fluttered from his hands, and the entirety of his pulped head decorated the back of the counter in gore. His body slumped to the floor and was virtually headless. Only a large flap of skin hanging from his gushing neck wound was still holding any remnants of his face, with half his mouth and nose still attached.

Behind them, the room continued to fill with a cloud of icy smoke that leaked from within the freezers, the shots having pierced the sealed coils inside. Leaking the chlorofluorocarbons into a hazy, dreamlike mist.

Still heaped on the cop's feet in a daze, the junkie managed to look up through the pain from his freshly cracked skull. He had witnessed what happened even if he could not believe it. Clumsily, he staggered to his feet, the blood gushing down his forehead.

"What did you do that for?" he slurred, unable to clear the blurriness from his eyes, the trembling in his body or the imbalance in his gait.

The cop didn't reply. He simply leaned forward and thrust the shotgun into the arms of the shocked junkie.

Gripping it instinctively in a shaky grip, this junkie may not have been that smart, but he knew he had to leave immediately. Whatever was happening was too confusing and surreal for him to comprehend. So, the junkie turned down the aisle and quickly headed toward the exit, intent on leaving and not looking back to the huge policeman.

. . .

Outside the 7-Eleven, car thirty-six had pulled up, and the two policemen stood outside, waiting. A bleep of a siren grabbed their attention as car twenty-one quickly pulled up next to them.

"'Bout goddamn time," the rotund cop muttered to his partner.

Right at that moment, the door to the convenience store forcefully swung open, and the junkie almost fell as he raced out in a panic. Desperate to escape and with shotgun in hand, he looked petrified at the other cops. Pulled out of whatever high he was on, he stared in a daze, drenched in as much sheer terror as blood from his cracked head. He had no idea what was happening as he staggered away from the door in front of the store's large window.

"It was one of you," he shouted to the waiting cops in terror. "You killed that guy, not me. I'm innocent!"

The junkie was in such a cloud he did not hear the warnings being shouted to him. He did not hear the call to put down the gun, or they would fire at him. The junkie was just getting more and more agitated. "It's happening again!" he screamed out as the pain in his head wound had become an increasingly pounding force. "It was a cop!"

He could not focus from panic, so he had no idea that the cops drew their guns and issued one last warning. He just waved the shotgun around, trying to escape the pain and confusion, screaming about a killer cop.

The police fired in unison. All four cops unloading their weapons.

The junkie's body was forced backward as the barrage of bullets struck his chest, sending him crashing through the window behind him, shattering the glass as he tumbled back into the store.

The freezer mist had almost filled the store and, with the window broken, crept out onto the sidewalk.

Over the next few minutes, the four policemen had entered the store, guns raised as they searched the hazy scene for other possible armed suspects. But all they found was the headless body of the clerk behind the counter, lying in a pile of losing, blood-soaked lottery tickets.

"You think I wanted to get this job?" Police Commissioner Doyle said in a fluster. "Pike gets offed by that maniac cop, and I get thrown into bullshit nonsense about Matt Cordell?"

Edward Doyle was too old for this. In his sixties, a competent politician, not to mention ex-captain of the NYPD, he had been very happy where he was as a deputy police commissioner. He had no want to take on any higher mantel before his retirement, but with Commissioner Pike gone, he had been given little choice. They had spent months trying to find a replacement, but when they couldn't, Doyle was given the role.

In his City Hall office, he stood in front of a large Christmas tree, adjusting some of the decorations. Behind him, two off-duty officers sat in the chairs by his desk, Jack Forrest and Teresa Mallory.

Doyle continued. "I know Cordell, and I know he's gone . . . Anyway, Officer Forrest and Officer Mallory, it may have taken eighteen months, but I can confirm, *finally*, that you've been cleared of any wrongdoing." He turned to look at them. "In fact, I have requested that you both receive commendations for your actions at the pier."

"Does that mean we're back on active duty again?" Teresa asked, hopeful.

Doyle shook his head. "Not just yet," he said. "But you both remain on full pay until such time as everything's in place, which is why you're both here."

"But what about Cordell?" she insisted.

Doyle sighed and walked back over to his desk. "The current swept away the killer you faced, but please, for the love of all that's holy in this shithole world, stop calling the guy Cordell! You realize this would have been put to bed months ago if it wasn't for all that crap you're saying?" He sat down and looked at them sternly, mainly at Teresa. "He died in '76 in Sing Sing, as well you know."

Teresa knew better than to argue, but she could not hear another dismissive argument from an official again. "With all due respect, no, he didn't. Cordell was still alive. The doctor there told us as much. And you didn't find a body in the river because he must have survived."

Doyle smirked. "Ah, yes, Doctor Gruber, the man you say you met but who, when I spoke to him, had no recollection of ever talking to you. Your name was in none of the visitor logs—"

"It's true. He's alive," Jack interjected.

"Mother of God," Doyle sighed loudly. "Every time I see you both, it always is the same. Now please, stop with the ghost stories. Let Cordell be dead!"

As Teresa went to say something else, Doyle raised his hand to her, silencing any further protest. "Now, if you let me, I'll tell you what's gonna happen," he said. "Before any return to active duty, you will both need to spend some time with Susan Riley."

"The police psychologist?" Teresa asked with a disapproving look.

"The one and the same," Doyle replied. "She has an excellent record of helping officers readjust after trauma. She—"

"We're not crazy, Commissioner," Jack cut in again.

"Of course not," Doyle affirmed. "But this is what has to happen, or you will not be coming back. Do you understand?" he paused for a moment before continuing. "So, you'll both have to have no less than six sessions with Miss Riley. And as she's a cop, too, you have my authority to speak to her about any confidential matters with this case."

"But, I . . ." She could see from Doyle's expression that this was not a discussion or anything that could be bargained.

"You're both down for three o'clock tomorrow," Doyle added. "Be there . . . both of you. No *ifs*, no *buts*, no bullshit excuses."

Chapter 2

As the sun set, the night drifted inland, sending its shadow across the city. Down in East Harlem, a scream rang out from the depths of a long blind alley. A scream that was quickly followed by the smash of breaking glass.

Down a rusted fire escape, a figure scrambled frantically down the steps. Soon getting to the lowest flight, without even waiting for the ladder to drop to the ground, the figure hurdled over the rail and off the edge of the escape, falling ten feet down onto a parked car. As they landed, the metal of the car's roof buckled under their weight.

In this thick darkness, the figure quickly pulled a weapon from their belt, then clambered off from the crushed car. Walking, their leg bucked, having twisted their ankle in the fall. With a limp, they hobbled away.

Their pace quickly slowed as they looked around,

feeling that they may not be alone. With their gaze darting around, they stared at the surrounding shadows intently, trying to discern any shapes hidden within.

Seeing nothing, they took a tentative few steps forwarded, their grip tightening on their gun. The only sound they could hear was that of their own footsteps and panicked breaths.

Then . . .

Something . . .

There was something in the shadows ahead.

As they stopped again, their blood ran cold.

They raised their gun, unsure. Just getting the feeling of something amiss. But their effort was not sure enough as a shot rang out from the darkest shadows ahead.

Hitting them through their breastplate, they fell to the ground, and as they did, their finger pulled on the trigger of their gun. A shot loosed into the darkness.

With a smirk and a confident strut, Detective Lieutenant Sean McKinney stepped out of the shadows. Wearing a long raincoat, a wide-brimmed fedora, and police badge clipped to his belt, he looked every bit the stereotype of a detective as you could imagine. His skin was pock-marked and was as rough as leather, and he commanded respect just with a single look. In his late forties, he was tough as nails. With no wife or family, his whole identity was his job in the NYPD and had been since he joined the force in 1966.

Walking over to the body, he looked down with a

victorious smirk. The man he had shot was very much dead, the bullet having blasted through his heart. He was a greasy-looking rat of a man, covered in tattoos. Nearly all of which were white supremacist-themed. He also had a wealth of puncture wounds tracing up the insides of both of his arms and dried blood on his T-shirt. Not his own blood. The blood of three children that he had done the most unspeakable things to before McKinney had broken through his front door.

A pair of bright lights then shone into the alley as a car pulled up to its mouth, its headlamps blinding in. Illuminating the whole scene in their harsh glow.

"Police, freeze!" a voice commanded over the car's speaker.

McKinney squinted in the glare as he unclipped the badge from his belt. He held it up to what he could clearly recognize as a police cruiser. He watched as an officer and his partner got out and walked toward him, flashlights in their hands.

"Couldn't just wait for us, could ya, McKinney?"

McKinney shrugged and glanced back down to his handiwork.

"Hey, you okay?" the other officer asked.

McKinney nodded. "Never better."

"But you're shot!"

Looking down at his coat, McKinney noticed he had, indeed, been shot. The criminal's bullet must have grazed past when he fired into the shadows, cutting through his jacket. He had felt something on his arm but dismissed it at the time. "Huh, guess you're right," he muttered nonchalantly as he glared down at the dead man. "You ruined a damn good coat, you asshole."

"You could have waited for backup," the first officer said.

McKinney didn't reply.

The first sergeant then continued. "Too bad you had to cut him down. He would have been sent down for life."

"Sure, I guess," McKinney mumbled. "I got so much fucking paperwork to do now." Without another word, he turned and walked out of the alley, leaving the officers staring at each other, confused and somewhat intimidated by the man.

Less than twelve hours later, McKinney was sitting in the office of a police counselor. Having been ordered to have an appointment by his commander, he was not too happy about being here. But he had no way to avoid it. In the previous year, a new ruling had come in that all officers involved in any homicide had a mandatory requirement to attend a psychiatric evaluation before returning to duty.

McKinney did not want any part of it. He was so old school that if he did ever need to kill someone in the line of duty, he would just have an extra measure of booze before bed. Now, though, he was faced with having to talk about his feelings. Something he wouldn't even do to himself, let alone with a stranger.

Opposite, a woman in her late twenties, Susan Riley, sat with an open notebook in her hand. "I sense some reluctance with you, Detective," she said. "Have you had one of these sessions before?"

McKinney smiled, turning on his charm as best as he could. "First, it's Detective Lieutenant, and second, I haven't been to confession in nearly forty years."

Susan smiled politely, ignoring his attitude. "Would you care to tell me about the shooting, Detective Lieutenant?"

"Look, Doc, let's save time, shall we? You're gonna ask me about all my feelings . . . Well, I feel great about what I did. Damn great. I'm only sorry I didn't shoot him a few more times. Scum like that are a stain on this city . . . You see what he did to those kids? So, does me liking what I did to an evil POS make me crazy, or are the lawyers and the judges the crazy ones 'cause they put that pedo prick back out on the streets. Just cause of a dumb technicality? He got back out and took three more kids! So, yeah, I'm glad he's dead, glad I did it. Glad I shot him in his black heart. Case closed. So, what do you think about that, Doc?"

"Well," Susan replied, unfazed by his rant, "firstly, Detective Lieutenant, I am not a doctor but a clinical psychologist. So, you can call me Miss Riley or Susan. Secondly, are you wanting me to log that you are here under protest?"

McKinney nodded, "Yeah, I am . . . So, how long does my ass have to warm this chair to satisfy this bullshit 'mandatory requirement'?"

"Every officer involved in a homicide, even one that you see as deserved, sees a counselor. At least one appointment, for us to determine any potential negative side effects from the incident you were involved in. And the more you fight against it, the longer it will all take for me to sign you off."

"Sure," McKinney said with a sigh, not agreeing at all. "Look, Miss Riley, I'm sure all your hippy-dippy peace-and-love bullshit will work with some shmoes, but I think I'm cured. So, thank you so much for your time. I'll see myself out." Getting up, he started for the door.

"Excuse me, Detective Lieutenant, didn't you have a partner? Sergeant Joseph Minella."

Stopping in his tracks, McKinney turned to her with a curious expression. "Sure. Joe and I were a team. Why?"

"He had an appointment with me once. About six months ago. He phoned and requested my help . . . That's unusual, isn't it? A cop asking that?"

"Not really," McKinney answered. "Joe was kind of a . . . sensitive guy. What did he want help with?"

"I never got to find out. He stood me up. Never showed. That was a Friday. The following night, he committed suicide with his service revolver."

"Yeah, I found his body the Monday after. What's your point?"

"You found him? I didn't know that . . . Anyway, someone must have talked Joe out of coming here. Probably told him he'd be a wimp if he admitted something was bothering him. Am I close?"

McKinney smiled but was angry, expertly masking all he wanted to say. "Well, that's a theory."

Susan's gaze was as strong and unwavering as his as she added, "How do you feel about me saying all that, insinuating you could have been the cause. Do you feel like screaming? Crying? Shooting me?"

"I see what you're doing, and I commend it." He opened the door and turned to leave. "Nice tactic to get me to open up. But I won't bite."

"Please don't slam the door," she added.

But he did not slam it, he just left it wide open after walking out.

Out of the office and through the reception office, McKinney strode past two off-duty officers who were silently waiting: Jack Forrest and Teresa Mallory. Without even a glance their way, he pushed through the glass doors and exited the building.

From inside the counselor's office, Susan peered out. "Jack Forrest and Teresa Mallory? Please come in."

· · ·

Without missing a beat, Susan was behind her desk and continuing with her next appointment. Her unsatisfactory appointment with Detective Lieutenant McKinney had not gone well, but it was never going to, not with a man so stuck in a machismo frame of mind. A man who shut all feelings out. She knew that. She knew exactly what kind of man he was and knew that the shooting he was involved in had not affected him at all. So, she would sign him back to work even after their short time together.

Teresa looked nervous after having been talking to Susan for thirty minutes and had an uphill battle trying to answer her questions.

"Are you going to find us unfit for the job?" Teresa asked bluntly.

"I hope not," Susan replied. "But how do you both feel about it? Do you think you're ready for being back?"

"We're both as sane as you are," Jack stated.

"It's not really about sanity," Susan replied. "It's about trauma-induced delusion. We know Matthew Cordell was buried a long time ago. That is on record, and no one who you talked to corroborated your side of the story. And no witnesses back up who you think did it."

"We both saw him on the Pier 18 months ago. I even got his badge from him that has his name as clear as day," Jack replied. "So, even with all you denying it, both Teresa and I know what and who we saw. And that doesn't make us nuts."

Susan nodded. "You saw a large man whose face was horribly disfigured. Correct?"

"Yes," Teresa confirmed.

"And he wore a police issue badge that said Cordell on it?"

"Yes," Teresa repeated.

"Did he ever say he was Matthew Cordell? Speak as if he were him?"

"No. He never spoke," Jack replied.

"So, let me put this to you," Susan began. "He could've been anyone in a policeman's uniform. Could have fabricated a badge. Could be someone trying to pretend to be Cordell. Doesn't that make more sense than a dead man coming back to kill New Yorkers?"

Jack had reached his limit, trying to convince anyone of what they saw. "Hey, if that's the official line the department wants to take . . . great. I'm all for it."

"No, Jack," Teresa protested. "It's a lie. I know it was him. *You* know it was!"

Jack looked to her, his eyes apologetic. "I love you. You know I do. But I need to be a cop. It's not just my job—it's my life. What the hell's the difference *who* he really was? We can think of one thing but don't have to broadcast it. He's gone. It's all over."

"We have to tell people because he's coming back. They never found a body because he didn't die." Teresa looked at Jack and Susan in turn. "Because you can't kill the dead . . . This zombie can't even be shot in the head. We have to warn people. If we don't, so many could die. Maybe not today, maybe in a decade. But he will, at some point . . . And I—" She stood, having let her emotion get the better of her, and did not want to allow that any more. She shook her head and walked out of the office, holding back the tears.

Jack looked to Susan with a worried expression. "Don't quote her on that, okay? Let me talk to her. I'll make her see some sense."

Susan put her notepad down and leaned forward. "I have to tell you . . . my evaluation of her has to be negative. The NYPD can't put anyone out on the street with a gun who has emotional problems, delusion, or anything that could impair her judgment. And she was basically saying that the dead came back. A zombie that will come back to get everyone. I know you believe it was Cordell, too, but you have to see how it all sounds like a fantasy."

"I wanna be crystal clear," Jack said. "I *am* saying it was Cordell, not that he was a zombie. I've seen smack heads do a lot of damage after being shot in the brain, so I'm not saying any spooky shit went down. What I saw was insane, but I'm not hanging my rep on ghosty shit."

Susan nodded. "Which is why your evaluation may well have a very different outcome to Ms. Mallory's. She said the word zombie three times in this one meeting."

. . .

The rest of the day didn't go too well for Jack. Teresa screamed at him for an hour after their counseling appointment, accusing him of not backing her. Saying he was avoiding the truth about Cordell. Because of this argument, he propped himself at a bar for the rest of the evening, alone.

When last orders was eventually called and he was forced to leave, he began his long trek back to his apartment. The same apartment he had not changed a thing in since his wife had been murdered. All her clothes remained hanging in the closet. All her family photos hung in frames on the walls. It was like she had never left.

Having been accused of her murder, he was grateful he finally received the official word that it was over. That the ghosts that hung over him were gone. That people who knew of the allegations against him would stop glaring at him. They would no longer whisper in corridors about how they were not surprised and they always thought he could be a murderer. There was nothing like being accused of your wife's murder to really see who your friends were.

On the autumn streets, even wearing a six-beer-deep glaze, the chill on the street cut through Jack. Wearing only a thin windbreaker, he zipped it up fully and thrust his hands into his pockets, hoping to shield himself.

As he climbed the stairs at the elevated train entrance, he longed for sleep. Not long to go. After a ten-minute train ride, he would be in throwing distance of his bed. He then pledged to sort things out with Teresa the next day and would avoid drunk calling her right then.

For now, he would just enjoy his stupor.

Jack had traveled from this train station many, many times. So much so that the old blind man who ran the newsstand knew his name from the sound of his voice. And tonight, even at this hour, that news-stand was open.

"Bit late for you, Harry," Jack said to the old man.

Upon hearing his voice, Harry smiled. "That you, Jack?"

"Sure is."

"I hear congratulations are in order." As Harry spoke, his hand patted the counter for the pile of the latest editions of the *Evening Post*. "You got your picture on the front of the paper." After grabbing a copy from the pile, he handed the newspaper over. "I had a customer read it out for me." He grinned.

Jack's eyes widened as he looked at the front page. Even after eighteen months, people were still reporting on this, but for the first time, they had a photo of Jack, right there on the cover. "PATROLMAN INNO-CENT," the headline stated. And below, a subheading, "Officer Forrest cleared of wife's murder. Maniac Cop ruled the culprit."

Jack could not hide his smile. It hit hard seeing that in print. Even if he wasn't filled with booze, he would have still felt this wave of emotion. He thought he should frame this page. Frame it, then shove it up the asses of everyone who said *he* was the murderer, that he was the maniac on the loose.

"Can I get a dozen, Harry?" Jack asked as he fished in his pocket for some cash.

"The picture that good?" Harry smiled as he started to count twelve editions off from the pile.

"How can it not be?" Jack laughed as he put a ten-dollar note on the counter.

Around them, the station was empty, which Jack soon noticed. "How come you're open?" he asked. "Seems dead. Don't you wanna just go home with a cold drink and warm woman?"

Harry shrugged. "As much as I'd love that, my warm woman passed away a long time ago." Handing over the dozen papers, his hand found the ten-dollar note. "This a ten?" he asked, knowing the answer from touch. He had a habit of checking with the customers, to see their honesty as some occasionally tried to game his blindness by paying with a single dollar they claimed was more.

"Yeah, keep the change." Jack smiled.

"Why, thank you."

"Now, let's see how good I come off in this," Jack muttered as he opened the paper and read the inner page.

Alongside the article, there were photos of the police van sitting at the abandoned pier, cordoned off with police tape. The same van he had been kidnapped in.

Next to that was a picture of his wife smiling. One that made a lump appear in Jacks's chest as he felt a sudden pang of grief.

But that emotional lump was quickly forgotten as a long stiletto blade shot through the paper he held, slicing into it through its center fold.

Looking down, Jack's surprise turned into a mortifying fear as he realized that the blade was not coming from in front but from behind him but *through* him. From his spine, through his heart and out of his chest, the tip of which, dripping with blood, had pierced the newspaper in his hands.

Harry's ears pricked up. He had no idea what just happened but heard a shuffle, followed by a gasp of breath. He did not see the huge, uniformed officer pull the knife out of Jack's back and ram it back it into him again and again. He did not see the officer hold Jack's limping body up by the back of his neck as he continued his assault.

The old blind man could only hear the wet *thwack, thwack, thwack* of the vicious attack, along with the muted *crack* as Jack's spine broke in through his body. The blade's hilt had rammed into that bone and split it in two.

The amount of hits, coupled with the strength of the officer, had broken a huge gaping, bloody hole in Jack's back. The officer then withdrew his blade and slammed Jack's head onto the counter in front. Blood spraying out, not just from the back wound but Jack's mouth and ears. Flying everywhere, staining the papers and shelves with a deep arterial red.

"Jack?" Harry called out, scared at the sounds. "What's happening? What's that noise?"

The old man may have not been able to see, but he could smell better than most. And what he could smell did not need any honed senses. It was a reek of dampness and mold, mixed with the foulness of excrement and bile.

Reaching his hand across the counter, Harry tried to steady himself. He had no idea what he would find but did not expect his fingers to brush against a huge, clenched fist, covered in a thin glove. A fist that quickly let go of Jack's hair and pulled away, leaving Harry's hand resting on a mass of blood-matted hair.

"Jack? Talk to me," Harry said in a panic as the warm wetness he touched made his stomach churn.

The train station began to rumble as an express train rushed between the platforms loudly, and as it did, the officer disappeared.

He left Jack's dead body, slumped face down over the counter. His eyes staring lifelessly at the floor below.

Harry's trembling hand traced down Jack's back and soon dipped into the large cavity caused by the repeated stabbing. As the blind man felt part of an extruding spine, he gasped and yanked his hand back.

"Help me!" Harry immediately shouted. He did not know if whoever did this to Jack was still around, but he couldn't do nothing. He had to try and call attention to the empty station. "Police!" he shouted even louder.

But the attacker had left, disappeared without a trace. The only evidence of his presence was the bloodied, mutilated remains of Officer Jack Forrest.

"Police! Police! Police!" Harry kept crying out, hoping someone would hear his pleas.

Detective Lovejoy waited in the morgue.

Despite years of working homicide, he had never become accustomed to the sight of blood and death. He'd always told himself that time would dull his revulsion, but it never had. Ever since he was an eight-year-old boy, led to a funeral home to see his grandmother's body, it had been that way. His mother had insisted he kiss that cold, lifeless cheek, and from that single moment, something inside him recoiled at anything remotely connected to the dead.

The squeaking of the trolley being wheeled into the room grated on his nerves as he peered up and saw the medical examiner bringing in a corpse under a white sheet.

"You look as well as ever, Lovejoy," the examiner chuckled.

"And you're one funny fucker," Lovejoy sneered back.

The examiner shook his head as he hit the brakes on the cart. "I swear they do this to you on purpose. Give you all the grossest cases."

Lovejoy couldn't help but agree. Throughout his career, he'd made countless attempts to avoid duties that involved the morgue or the crime scenes. He'd petitioned, pleaded, and practically begged for more office-based assignments, but his requests were always denied. But in his fifties, with years of service behind him, he had hoped he'd finally earned some reprieve. Yet here he was, waiting to see more of the reality he'd tried so hard to avoid.

The door to the morgue opened, and through it, Detective Lieutenant Sean McKinney walked in, followed by Teresa Mallory. With bloodshot eyes and looking emotionally drained, she had taken the news of Jack's murder bad. Very bad.

Without even a hello, McKinney motioned blankly at Lovejoy. "Remove the sheet."

"Oh, fuck no. You do it," Lovejoy grumbled as he stepped away from the gurney.

With a smirk, McKinney leaned forward, grabbed a corner of the white sheet, and pulled it back.

On his back and with the blood cleaned off, Jack's catastrophic injuries were hidden below, all aside from the two dozen puncture wounds at the front of the chest. The top one of which peeked out under the edge of the blanket. But all bruising was minimum, and the blood was gone, every wound dry.

As Teresa saw Jack's face, she almost cried out.

McKinney placed a hand on her shoulder. As comforting as he would ever get.

The examiner nodded before walking over to another table, where two detectives stood next to the body of a young redhead. With no sheet for vanity, her naked body was being laid out clinically as the examiner and detectives discussed her death in hushed tones.

Back with McKinney, he had always tried to tread carefully with the grieving, but he was a bull in a china shop ninety-nine percent of the time. He looked at Teresa and attempted speaking a calm and kind tone, but his words never came out in the best way.

"Did he ever mention what he wants done with his corpse?"

Teresa shook her head, gritting her teeth to stop the tears from coming. "I'll call his mother in Florida. She might want him there."

Lovejoy had zoned out, but he soon overheard the medical examiner speaking about the body of the redhead.

"Cause of death was strangulation, like all the others. All strippers." The examiner sighed. "Sure picks the pretty ones, though . . . And from her bruising, she put up one hell of a fight."

Lovejoy grimaced, trying to ignore the sick feeling in his throat as he turned back to the case at hand.

"Can you think of anybody with a motive to kill Jack?" McKinney asked.

Teresa stared at him. "Really? After all we've been through, you go to that?"

"Well, you were seen having an argument in the precinct cafeteria yesterday. You stormed out, right? You were angry? Where did you go?"

"Home."

"Okay, you went home." McKinney nodded. "And you didn't wait outside the bar for him later on? To make up or go for round two?"

Teresa took a breath before answering, not breaking her eye contact with the blunt detective. "I went home. I stayed at home."

"I'm just playin' devil's advocate, but you could've easily waited till he finished at the bar and caught up with him at the train station."

Behind them, a long mirror stretched the length of the room, and with one glance at it, Teresa knew full well what was happening. That was a one-way mirror, leading to an observation room. These were not just harmless questions, but she was being interrogated and behind the glass was most likely Commissioner Doyle, who wanted all of her story swept under the rug.

Ignoring the mirror, she turned to McKinney. "I'd have no reason to kill Jack. I loved him."

Well, according to the counselor you both saw, he didn't one-hundred-percent believe your theory on what happened with that maniac cop. So, maybe he had enough? Wanted out? You couldn't have that?"

With a sudden flush of rage, Teresa could not stop her hand from moving to strike McKinney across the face. But he knew it was coming and had engineered the situation. He managed to move in time and grab her by the wrist before the slap landed.

"Jesus, you're strong. I can barely hold you," he said. Still keeping a grip on her. Stopping her from pulling her hand back. "It would have taken a strong woman to plunge a knife that deep into his back, a *very* strong woman."

Yanking her arm away, she glanced at Lovejoy, who just stood by, distracted by the other case in the room.

"This is *bullshit*, and you know it," Teresa shouted. "You've been a detective long enough to smell when something's wrong. Why don't you ask Doyle who killed Jack?" She then shot the mirror a harsh glare, knowing the commissioner was in there watching. "He knows. We told him we were in danger."

"I'm just following procedure," McKinney said. "You know that the prime suspects are always relatives, close friends, or lovers. Nine out of ten times, you find the killer among those groups."

"Not when Matthew Cordell's involved," she shot back, trying her best to not scream at him in fury.

Behind the glass, it was not just Commissioner Doyle who was there, who was watching everything that was happening in the morgue, but also Susan Riley. And when Teresa had mentioned Matthew Cordell, she noticed the commissioner's sudden look of unease. Something more than just not believing her. But a palpable fear.

Teresa could not take it any longer as she stormed out of the room, her head a buzz of anger and grief. She had to leave before she did something she would regret.

McKinney turned to Lovejoy. "Go after her. See where she goes."

Lovejoy, not wanting to be around death anymore, simply nodded and followed her out of the door.

After a few moments, across the far side of the room, the examiner and other detectives were still busily discussing their strangulation case as, from a nearby side door, Commissioner Doyle and Susan Riley walked in from the observation room.

McKinney walked over to meet them. "I don't like what you're asking me to do with this Mallory girl," he said, knowing full well she could not have been the killer.

Doyle replied in a monotone. "It's for the good of the department more than just this case." He then looked down at Jack's body with distaste. "I really don't consider her a suspect. It's just a way to put her on the defensive for a while. Keep her under control and, most of all, away from reporters. Last thing we need is all that maniac cop nonsense coming to haunt us. The papers are only just starting to leave that subject alone."

"Maniac cop nonsense?" McKinney sneered as he repeated. "I had friends *murdered* by that guy. It was not nonsense."

"I didn't mean it like that," Doyle said dismissively. "Anyway, you need to keep the pressure on her. That's a direct order. Got it?"

"Our time would be better spent finding out who did this," McKinney retorted, pointing to Jack's corpse.

Without replying, Doyle walked back through the side door. Ending the conversation rudely. Leaving Susan Riley with him.

McKinney turned to her. She was standing there, looking uncomfortable. "I don't like any of this either," she said.

"Your report described her as mentally unsound and unfit for duty," he retorted.

"I know, but how can I really judge her? She's out there taking the heat . . . being a cop. I'm behind a desk, like a social worker. Judging her by one meeting."

Commissioner Doyle was back in the observation room with his head in his hands. He did not know what to do. He had been thrust into this position, with no warning or handover. He was standing in a dead man's shoes, trying to fix the NYPD, trying to avert any more riots or murders. If he was brave enough, he would admit that he had no real idea what he was doing and was making it up as he went along. But also, he could not let anyone believe it was Cordell.

Leaving the morgue, McKinney and Susan walked along the corridor toward the exit.

"No offense," he said. "I just don't like people that try and get inside other people's heads."

Susan smiled. "You made that obvious enough in my office. Any reason?"

"I'll tell you this . . . My wife was under a psychiatrist's care for a year. Standard problems, you know? She was a cop's wife . . . Pretty soon, she couldn't get along without him. She couldn't even talk to me about anything. Had to talk to him first." He stopped in his tracks to look at her. "Now, she's my ex-wife. He convinced her she was better off without the marriage. That a good enough answer?"

"Is that true?" she asked, sensing he had just made it up on the spot.

"Possibly," McKinney answered with a smile.

Susan rushed a few steps to keep up. "So, you think Commissioner Doyle is trying to hide something?"

"You said it, not me." After a beat, he stopped clearly perturbed by his sudden thought. He turned to her with a sudden flash of annoyance.

Chapter 3

The elevated train station had reopened in only a matter of hours after the mauled body of Jack Forrest had been removed. The sheer amount of spilled blood had been left soaking into the newspapers and magazines, pooling down onto the concrete floor. Harry, the owner, had been told by the police that cleaning up the area was down to the sanitation department. But they refused to send anyone and claimed it was the responsibility of the business owner . . . him.

So, the old, blind man had spent the first few hours of the day throwing away most of his stock as well as hosing the floor down, hoping he had got all of the blood. No one stopped to help. No one stopped to even buy a paper. They just saw the blood and hurried by, disgusted.

The rest of the day had been spent with people

complaining about how there was still patches of red staining some magazines or that the place smelled of copper. But what could he do? So, he just sat behind his counter and hoped that this, like most bad things in his life, would soon pass.

From behind his counter, he could hear the footsteps of commuters walking by but had heard one particular set. A pair of heels, walking up and standing there, not saying a thing. He gave her a few moments until he eventually spoke up. "Can I help you, miss?"

"How do you know I'm a miss?" Susan replied.

"Well, if you were a man in heels like yours, I presume you would prefer for me to call you miss as well." Harry shrugged. "You've been here a while. You looking for anything in particular?"

"I'd like to talk to you, if that's okay?"

"Do I know you?"

"No," Susan replied. "I'm with the police department."

Harry sighed. "I've got nothing to say. I've spoken to enough of you guys already. And not one of you helped me clean this place up. Left it covered in blood and . . . Ah, you don't wanna hear about this."

Susan looked at the stand around the magazines and could see red specks. Red what must have been a powerful spray of blood across it. "I'm not an investigator like the others," she continued. "I'm a psychologist, trying to get a profile on the person who was here."

"As I said, I've got nothing to say," Harry repeated. "I'm trying to make a living here."

"Okay, that's fair, but how about I make you a deal?"

Harry leaned forward. "I'm not into women if that's what you're offering," he chuckled.

"Ah, well, my loss," Susan laughed. "How about, instead, I get all the magazines off the shelves that still have blood on them? Would you talk then?"

Without a second thought, Harry nodded. "Yes, I would."

"Okay."

And with that, Susan walked over to the side of the stand and began to take out every paper or magazine or postcard that had any traces of the violence from the previous night. She was not squeamish at all. Though she knew the person who had died here, she could disassociate enough to pick up a few spattered publications. While she was piling them up in her arms, she allowed other commuters to come in and grab their papers, pay, then leave.

When she was done, she had nearly thirty magazines and papers piled on the counter.

"There," she said. "Rest all seem clean."

Feeling the pile with his hands, Harry looked surprised. "That many? Poor guy didn't stand a chance, did he." Lifting the soiled pile off the counter, Harry placed them underneath. "Well, a deal's a deal," he continued. "Ask away."

"Could you tell from his footsteps if he was a large man? Perhaps he said something?"

Harry shook his head. "No footsteps, which was weird. I always hear people. Anyway, that's all in the police report. I just heard Jack screaming and the stabbing . . . . That's all—and then the blood, it covered me, you know?"

Susan knew it was a long shot to come here. She was just about to say thank you, then leave, when he suddenly remembered something.

"Wait, I do remember one thing . . . I touched him."

Susan's eyes widened. "The killer?"

With a nod, Harry's tone became graver. "It sounds stupid. But you see, I lost my sight in combat in Sicily back in the war. A Nazi grenade went off in my face. Killed all the others in the foxhole around me . . . . I lay there more than four days, surrounded by their bodies. Hiding. Waiting for the bastards to leave. Buried in among my friends' blood and guts . . ." His brow furrowed as he remembered. "The days were hot and the nights so, so cold. But them being on top of me kept me from freezing to death . . . You never forget the feeling of cold, dead flesh."

A train shot by the station, and when it did, Harry fell silent, waiting for it to pass. Waiting for the noise of it to settle.

Susan was on tenterhooks, waiting for a punchline that she did not know whether she was ready to hear.

When it passed, Harry immediately continued. "I

never thought I'd feel anything like that again. Then I touched what I think was that guy's hand. Just for a second, mind you, and I was back there again . . . with the dead. It wasn't his skin I touched as well. He had a glove on. But the fabric was really thin. I could even feel his coldness beneath that. Before you just call me crazy and say I had cold fingers, there was something else about him. His smell. He had that smell of death. Imagine what a dead body smells like after it sits in the sun all day, then grow cold, then heats up. The body voids itself when it dies. See, did you know that? Then the meat of the body starts to decay and putrefy. Not to mention the smells inside the body that leak that out through the wounds."

"What does that smell like?" she asked.

"Like rot and mold and shit and vomit all rolled into one."

Susan's mind spun as she left the newsstand. She had heard tall tales of delusion before, and she thought she was a good judge of a person. She had a nose for telling if someone was telling the truth or at least believed in what they said, even if was not true. With Teresa, her emotional reactions led her to believe that it was her making herself believe her stories. But now, with this old man, he had believed it too. This did not mean Susan was a believer in Matthew Cordell being a zombie back for revenge but that there was a lot more to this than the commissioner had let on. If not what they thought, it could be a very elaborate ruse, put into motion for an unknown reason.

Across the other side of Manhattan, a man in his thirties sprinted up an otherwise quiet, residential street. He wore a pair of finely pressed khakis and a crisp flannel shirt. The expression on his perfectly shaven face was a chaotic blend of agitation and panic as he ran toward this car.

"Hey, stop!" he yelled, his voice high with desperation. "Goddammit. Don't do that, come on!"

But his pleas had come too late. The large tow truck had already maneuvered into position, its massive hook clanked into place, latching onto the front of the man's gleaming, high-end Mercedes. The hydraulics of the truck roared to life with a mechanical whine, and in one smooth, unrelenting motion, the front of the car was suddenly lifted into the air as the truck prepared to haul it away.

"Aw, for God's sake, why? I'm here now!" the man exclaimed, arriving at the scene out of breath. "Shit, shit, shit! This can't be happening to me."

The driver of the van, a traffic enforcement agent, was a thick-necked, intransigent, barrel-chested man who chomped on his stogie as he went to lock the tow hook into place. He was dressed in a dark blue uniform, stained with oil and scuffed from years of work. Over it, he wore a bright, high-vis vest. Bold letters printed across its back read *NYPD Traffic*. On the breast of this jacket was an embroidered name badge that simply read *Bud*.

He was a man who had towed hundreds of cars. From accidents to ones violating parking rules. And in doing so for the latter, he had heard excuse after excuse from all kinds of people trying to justify how their illegal parking should be excused, and not once did he ever relent to their demands, pleas, or threats. Nowadays, he barely flinched at the yelling aimed at him. He just carried on with what he was supposed to do. To this traffic officer, the Mercedes was just another car driven by another asshole on another day on Manhattan's streets.

Turning to the angry and upset man, Bud handed him a folded piece of paper. "This is for you," he grunted.

Taking the paper, the man opened it up and saw the words *Parking Violation Summons* printed above the seal of the City of New York.

"Ticket number, violation details, and instructions on how to respond are all on there." His gravelly voice reeled off the spiel as he had done many times before. Barely even thinking of what he actually said anymore. "You plead guilty and pay the fine or contest the violation by scheduling a hearing. Payment details are also listed, along with the further information of noncompliance consequences and where your car will be impounded."

The man stared at the paper in shock. "Come on. Can't we just talk about this? I was just coming back to move it anyway. I'm here now."

"Well, I got here first," Bud replied as he tried locking the hook into place once more. But it was not catching.

"But I'm *right here!*" the man pleaded. "You can't take it away now that I'm here."

"Read the summons," Bud replied as he tried to fix the lock again. Stepping closer, he clicked it in place, and as quickly as it clipped it, it unclipped again. "Shit," he grumbled.

The man turned up and down the dusky street-lamp-lit street and noticed they were the only people there. "Hey, look, pal. There's no one else here. How about we work this out between us, yeah? I got a crisp hundred-dollar bill that—"

Bud, still trying to fix the safety clip in place, turned to the man with a look of annoyance. "You tryin' to offer me a bribe?" he asked, exhaling stogie smoke that billowed up around his stubbly jaw.

"Oh no . . . Not at all!" the man replied with a sudden shock of nervousness. "But if you take my car, I won't be able to get to work tomorrow. I'll lose the whole day. I'll lose money."

Bud grunted with amusement. "Yeah, you can afford it."

The man's nervy yet polite demeanor then dropped to one of annoyance. "You enjoy this, don't you? You son of a bitch . . . You've got this shitty civil service job, and you love your little power plays, huh? You get off on this, don't you?"

Bud grinned as the man broke and showed his true self. He took another puff on his stogie and went back to trying to fix the lock on the hook. He grabbed the hydraulic controls again to raise the car a bit higher.

But the khaki-dressed man was not finished. "You'll never be *anything*. You'll be towing cars the rest of your goddamn life. And for what? I'm offering you a hundred bucks to look the other way, which you probably don't earn in a day."

Pressing the red button, the hook whirred loudly as it pulled the car off the ground a few more, and as it did, the metal of the Mercedes groaned under its own weight.

"Careful, you asshole!" the man bellowed. "I just had it detailed!"

Bud, not caring at all for the man or his car, took the loose chain that dangled in front of him, then swung it back and onto the bonnet of the car. The metal scraped across the paintwork as it landed.

"Motherfucker!" the man chided. "You can't even do this dumb, nothing job well . . . I'm gonna sue you, sue the city. Yeah. I know lawyers! Big fucking lawyers who would ruin you!"

Bud didn't care at all about the threats. The man

was in the wrong. He only cared that at this higher angle, the lock for the hook would not stay in place. He was damned if he would let this man beat him. Not here, not tonight.

Bud looked at the man. "You better start thinking about getting out to Brooklyn early tomorrow to reclaim this heap," he said, taking the stogie out of his mouth to point at the man, enjoying the chance to rile him more. "A lot of cars get stripped in our lot, the stereo, the tires, even the engine now and then. That's why I don't own a car. So, get there first thing. We open at six."

Just as the man was about to scream more threats at Bud, a shadow fell across both of them.

Turning, the man gasped in surprise at the sudden appearance of this tall police officer. He did not see the water damage to the fabric or smell the foul odor coming off the man. He only saw the uniform, and he got scared, knowing that insulting any city official could be seen as verbal assault and an arrestable offense.

"Uh, hi, Officer. I wasn't going to start anything," the man started, babbling. "I bet he gets cursed out all day, every day, right?" He turned to Bud and forced a smile. "You don't care, right? It's part of the job. All in good fun, yeah?"

But Bud did not see the uniform. He saw a much more horrible sight. He saw the man's monstrous face staring down at them.

Without warning, the cop struck Bud across the side of the head with his billy club. A force so hard it immediately cracked Bud's skull inward. A two-inch wide break in his cranium that started to jettison blood and brain matter from within.

Bud immediately fell to the asphalt as he tried to speak, tried to scream, but all that came out was a mix of slurred words. "Why . . . Help . . . Ma . . . Ma . . . Ma . . ."

After a few seconds, the cop grabbed Bud's rotund body by the overalls and lifted him up with one hand, off the concrete. With his other hand, the cop reached over and wrenched the hook from off of the Mercedes, sending the car falling back down to the street with a loud crash. He then took that hook and rammed it into Bud's convulsing body through his chest.

Slamming on the hydraulic button, the hook wound up higher, wrenching Bud's body upward as he weakly called for his mother, and his blood pumped out of his head in jets at a horrifying speed.

"Ma . . . Ma . . . Ma . . ."

The man was frozen, unable to move from the sheer surreal violence of what had happened. None of this could be real. It *couldn't* be. Even the blood that soaked his khakis was not enough to force him into running. He was too scared.

With Bud dangling from his own tow truck's hook in his chest, convulsing uncontrollably as the last of his life ebbed away, emitting only pained groans without words, the door to the truck slammed shut. With a roar of the engine and a screech of tires, the truck lurched forward as it sped down the empty street, Bud's body hanging from the winch bar like some sick trophy of the hunt.

The truck soon rounded a corner up ahead and was gone, the noise taken with it.

Staring after the tow truck, the man found himself helpless for a few moments. Unsure and unable to move, until finally, he blinked, pulled from his paralysis. His face was racked in utter shock as he looked at the summons in his hand and let it go as soon as he noticed the blood that had sprayed upon it.

Trembling, he walked over to his car and opened the door. Not knowing what else he could do, he got in and drove home.

In the early hours of the following day as the sun breached the skyline, two NYPD squad cars pulled up outside a brownstone in Tribeca.

Within minutes, the owner of the house was dragged out, screaming from his front door and thrown onto the street by four police officers, right in front of his Mercedes.

"You killed him. Admit it!" one officer shouted as he kicked the man in the gut.

"No!" The man coughed loudly, tears streaming down his face.

He had gotten home last night to his expensive, empty house. He had tried to cook himself dinner but had, instead, ended up sitting on the floor of his shower, fully clothed as the warm water fell upon him, crying for hours. He did not know what he could do after what he witnessed and with the police at his door, beating him, he knew even less.

"He just gave me a ticket," he cried out. "Then . . . then this man." He wanted to explain. But who would believe him? The monster had come from nowhere and had managed to detach the hook from his Mercedes with one hand, while the other held up the considerable weight of the traffic officer. None of it was possible.

Yanking him up off the ground, a second officer slammed the man into the side of their squad car. "If not you, then who did it? Huh?"

"You won't believe me," the man whimpered as the new pain from the kick to his belly radiated throughout his body.

"Try me!" the officer replied.

"It . . . It was him . . ."

"Who?"

The man wept as he spoke. Remembering the killer. "It was this great big guy. A cop. Huge . . . Seven foot maybe . . ."

The other officers paused.

"You better not be fucking saying this," a third officer interjected.

Christian Francis

But the man continued, terrified. "He was scarred . . . never said a word . . . It was *him* . . . It was that maniac cop!"

Commissioner Doyle sat behind his office desk, his expression one of annoyance-tinged disapproval. Standing opposite him was Detective Lieutenant McKinney and the Chief of Police, Tom O'Hanlon.

"Just look at the reports," McKinney said to O'Hanlon as he pointed to the seven manila case file folders spread over Doyle's desk. "It's happening again, Chief."

"Gimme a break," O'Hanlon replied, rolling his eyes.

McKinney had no problem with authority. What he had a problem with were stupid people. "I'm talking about the man who killed your predecessor." He then motioned to the commissioner as well. "*Both* of your predecessors." He could not help but smile at how these men seemed to be blind to the glaringly obvious. "This is a guy who may try to pull the same shit again."

"Then, who else died on that pier?" O'Hanlon smirked. "Was that the wrong guy?"

"Are you kidding me?" McKinney sighed. "We have no body and a testimony that makes little fucking sense. So, it could be one of three things . . . The same guy, a guy who was in cahoots or a copycat. Either one of those things spells a shitload of problems for us. And you not seeing what's going on will only make this worse." He looked at Doyle to make sure he understood clearly what was being said. "When this leaks—and trust me, it will somehow—people are not gonna want to pick up the phone and dial 911. It'll be like before but way, way worse. Cos you assured them all it was all over. That they were safe."

O'Hanlon went to speak, but McKinney continued. "They're going to want to defend themselves as would any normal person. And if that happens, we're looking at a bloodbath. Citizens blowing cops as well as each other away . . . like there's no law."

"Oh, come on," Doyle said. "That's a bit exaggerated."

McKinney could not temper his voice as he shouted. "Don't you remember what happened? Even back then, people were killing out of fear. Remember that one woman who shot a damn security guard thinking it was the damn killer?"

"Tell me the truth," O'Hanlon said, keeping his tone even. "Do you really think it's a cop? Some officer that went off the deep end?"

Doyle shook his head. "He doesn't fit the description of any cop we have on the NYPD. Seven foot, with scars all over his face? I think that guy would stand out. We looked into every employee of the city. Turned up bubkes."

"Except one," McKinney said, deadpanning.

"Don't you dare." Doyle pointed sternly at him. "Don't even think it."

O'Hanlon stared at the commissioner, confused. "What are you both talking about? Was there a suspect?"

"Nothing. This is purely fantastical bullshit we have kept out of the papers," Doyle dismissed. "The only fact is we have to find this killer. Even if we have to put together a special task force or ask for aid from the governor or other agencies."

"The feds?" O'Hanlon asked, surprised.

Doyle nodded. "Maybe."

"We have a lead I wanna look into," McKinney suggested. "That officer, Teresa Mallory."

"Mallory?" Doyle laughed. "That nut job again?"

"Yeah, her." McKinney nodded. "The suspect killed her boyfriend, and I think it's quite probable that he could come after her next."

"If this is the same 'maniac cop' you're thinking of, and I don't think it is. He's had eighteen months," O'Hanlon said. "He could have killed this officer a long time ago, same with Officer Forrest. Why wait? If he was the same guy, wouldn't he had done it straight away?"

"I hate that name, Maniac Cop, like this is some trashy B movie," McKinney sighed. "As to why he waited? Well, that's something we'll need to ask him. Maybe he just likes fucking with people. Waiting till they least expect it. Or maybe when he fell into the

Hudson, he was badly hurt and needed time to heal. Lots of maybes."

Doyle collected all the folders from his desk into a pile and pushed them toward McKinney. "Maybe this is all just horseshit and is just another killer trying to make it look like that guy."

"Anything is possible." McKinney smirked. "I just hope he hasn't found her yet."

Chapter 4

Teresa's apartment was small, but it was all she could afford in walking distance to her precinct. Never wanting to commute, she paid nearly all of her meager officer's income on a shoebox home that consisted of an open-plan kitchen/living room/bedroom with a small separate bathroom. They called it a studio apartment, when, in fact, it was a converted store room with a bathroom attached. But even with its diminutive size, she had made this apartment her home. It was comfortable and safe. Now, though, with Jack having been taken violently away, nothing in this city felt even the slightest bit safe or comfortable anymore.

With a leather bag open on her bed, Teresa was busily packing an overnight change of clothes. She was done. Done with her job. Done with the city. Done with everything. She planned to leave as soon as she could, as soon as she could finish warning everyone.

She had not planned on the police counselor, Susan Riley, showing up at her door unannounced, insisting that they need to talk.

"I came here to tell you something," Susan said as she sat at the end of the bed, with Teresa continuing to pack. "I think I believe you. I don't know how or why, but I do."

"You shouldn't," Teresa sadly chuckled. "You'll be out of a job if you say that out loud."

Susan found this all hard. Not just saying sorry but realizing she was powerless in the situation. "I was asked by the commissioner to certify you unfit."

Teresa's expression was not surprised.

Susan continued. "But I can't do that . . . I've spent the day researching everything about Matthew Cordell. I know Detective Lieutenant has to. You're not on your own."

"If it's more information you want. There's a show on tonight called *Criminals At Large*. I'll be on it."

"That trash?" Susan was taken aback and couldn't tell if Teresa was serious. "You're kidding me, right?"

"Why not? They alert the public to wanted criminals."

"But it's just awful."

"A half dozen bad guys have been caught or turned in because of that awfulness." Pausing for a second, it was obvious that nerves were getting to her as she looked visibly shaky. "I don't know what else to do . . . I can't just run away and not warn people. The assholes in City Hall are covering it all up. And for what? Because of something that happened a decade ago? They want the story buried and me out of the picture. Well, I'm gonna make sure the story is told and then they'll get their second wish. I'll be gone and won't be coming back. I'm not staying in New York anymore."

"But if you go on that show, who's gonna believe it? The lunatic fringe?"

Teresa felt deflated. She did not trust this counselor, but there was no one else here for her. No friends, no family . . . no Jack. "Will you come with me?"

Susan already knew that whatever was going to happen it could mean career suicide for anyone involved. The commissioner would see to that. "Exactly what are you going to say?" she inquired.

Before Teresa could answer, a horn honked from the street below.

"That's my cab," she said. "I'm checking into a hotel tonight, then after this show's done. I'm packing up the rest of my stuff and leaving. As much as I can fit in a rental car."

"You think Cordell will be coming after you?" Susan said.

"He got Jack, so he's gonna look for me. Of course he is," Teresa said, picking up her bag and heading for the door.

"I'll ride with you," Susan offered as she followed Teresa out of the door, shutting it behind her.

. . .

With a single bag in her hand, Teresa stood in front of the empty taxi parked on the curb.

The sound of hurried, heavy footsteps stole their attention as a short and squat cabbie emerged from the nearby liquor store and jogged toward them, already out of breath from the exertion. Fishing out his keys from his jacket, he unlocked the car with a sheepish grin. "Sorry about that, ladies. Just needed a pack of smokes." He glanced at Teresa's bag. "That all you've got? Want me to toss it in the trunk?"

Teresa shook her head and opened the back door herself without a word. Susan nodded to the cabbie appreciatively.

Getting in the driver's seat, the cabbie flicked on the meter and looked at his passengers in the rearview. "Okay, ladies. Where to?"

Looking out of all the windows, Teresa checked for any sign of anyone. More specifically, anyone after her. When she could see that no one was around and the coast was clear, she spoke to the cabbie. "Mayflower Hotel."

Nodding, the cabbie turned the engine on, then pulled into the street. He glanced at her again in the rearview and could clearly see that she was nervous and still looking around for something. Wanting to lighten the mood, he grinned. "You know, lady. I saw you, then I saw the bag. I thought to myself, here's a ride to the airport! I'm usually spot on with that stuff. But can't win 'em all, huh? Just to the Mayflower!"

But Teresa was not engaging, especially as she noticed a car was behind them. Driving quite closely. "Pull over to the curb on the next corner, please," she said with a tremor in her voice.

"You see anyone?" Susan asked, confused, having not seen anything suspicious herself.

"Some ex givin' ya a hard time, eh?" the cabbie asked.

Teresa smiled politely. "Please, just pull over. Just for a second."

The cabbie, having heard many crazy stories and dealt with many crazy people, was not fazed in the slightest. "It's your dime," he said, pulling the cab over to a stop.

From behind, three cars zipped by.

After a few moments, and with a sigh of relief, Teresa nodded to the driver, who was watching her in his mirror, waiting for a cue.

With the evening traffic starting to build, more cars started to follow the cab's path. She did not see the suspicious vehicle following at great length behind them. A 1971 Police issue Plymouth Fury, painted two-tone black and white. And from within that car, there was a loud sound playing over the radio. Not music but the chatter of police calls.

But even though she did not see that vehicle, Teresa still looked nervous about all the car around her, something the cabbie noticed as he decided to turn off the main strip and down a side street.

"Where are you going?" Teresa worriedly asked.

"The shows are just letting out," he said. "So, there's gonna be loads of cars out on the street. We can beat some of the crosstown traffic on the backstreets. Less people here. Probably cut thirty minutes off our time avoiding the jams."

"Please stay on the busy streets," Teresa said, knowing that there was a safety in numbers.

"I think you should reconsider. You could be stuck in traffic for a while if ya d—"

Susan decided to step in and reached into her pocket, fishing out her police badge. Flashing it to the cabbie, she just repeated Teresa's words. "Please stay on the busy streets."

Nodding with a sigh, the cabbie looked forward again. "Fine, I'll loop back on the next block . . . but you're a cop, huh?"

"Both of us," Susan confirmed.

The cabbie sank into his seat. "Well, that means I ain't getting no tip," he grumbled. "None of you guys tip."

Teresa looked at Susan with some confusion. "You have a badge as a counselor?"

Susan smiled. "I know right, I'm *some* cop. Never arrested anybody. Never even worn my gun. I went straight into Internal Affairs 'cause of my psychology degree . . ."

As the cab turned onto the next street, getting to the edge of the warehouse district, the whole vehicle began to tremble slightly. The steering wheel shuddered in the cabbie's hands, prompting him to let out an annoyed groan.

"Ah shit, fuck, ass," he seethed under his breath, shooting a quick glance around the street ahead and pulling the taxi to the curb.

"What's the matter?" Teresa asked with a flash of panic. "Why are you stopping?"

"Think we got a flat," he said, stopping the car, then opening the door.

"No, stay in the car, please! *Stay in the car.*" Her eyes darted in every direction, scanning the fast-darkening streets around them. "Drive! Please!"

"Fuck no," he grunted. "Not ruining my rims."

"Take it easy," Susan said calmly to Teresa as she reached out and put a hand on her arm. "Anyone can get a flat. Nothing insidious."

"Cop or no cop, I own this thing," the cabbie said, getting out of the car. "I ain't ruining it for no one!"

Immediately, Teresa got out of the cab, too, looking around them, expecting the worst.

"We're not being followed," Susan said, shifting across her seat to follow Teresa. "You need to calm down."

Before she could get out of the cab, Teresa pushed Susan back onto the seat. "Stay in there," she sternly ordered.

The cabbie rolled his eyes as he crouched down beside the front driver side tire. It was pancake-flat. Standing up, he ambled around to the trunk. As he popped it, he noticed the rear left tire was also rapidly losing air. "What the hell did I drive over?" he muttered.

Teresa stared at the tires. "When you went for cigarettes, someone did this," she said.

"Freakin' kids," he exclaimed, throwing his arms in the air.

Over the cabbie's head, at a corner in the distance, a feeling of cold dread washed over Teresa as she saw a car sliding out into view. Slowly moving until the windshield could be seen and the person inside could see her, too.

"No," she whispered.

The cabbie began rooting around his messy trunk for the tire jack. But before he could find it or even realize what happened, the driver's door of the cab was slammed shut and the engine turned on.

"What the—"

The vehicle launched forward with a loud skid, peeling off down the street. Leaving him standing there with an expression of surprise.

"What are you doing?" Susan screamed from the back seat of the cab as it drove haphazardly down the street. You can't steal his car!"

Its flat tires dragged the car to one side as Teresa tried to compensate by steering the other way.

"*He's after me, not him,*" Teresa replied loudly as Susan bounced around in the back, trying to keep her balance, the open trunk flapping up and down, banging every time it shut and failed to lock in place.

Soon, this car was running on its rims, making an awful screech of metal dragging on concrete as she persisted in driving it.

Still standing in the middle of the dark street, lit by the newly illuminated streetlamp above, the cabbie's mouth was agape. He was in too much shock to be mad, but his anger was boiling rapidly to the surface.

Then, from behind, a black '70s police cruiser roared by at high speed. As if coming from nowhere, it took the cabbie by surprise, the wing mirror narrowly missing him by only a few inches.

Still in the warehouse district, the stolen cab was running lopsided on both rims of the flat tires. Sparks flew out from underneath as the metal painfully scraped along, the tires having been shredded off a few moments ago, leaving the strips of rubber far behind.

Out of the windshield, none of the surrounding buildings were open. All shopfronts were dark and closed up for the night. She could see that she had stayed on this street for too long and had, in her panic, driven further away from the busier parts of town. The safer parts.

The trunk still flapped open and closed with every bounce of the car, blocking Teresa's rear view in fits and starts. She was too focused on the road ahead to see the '70s police cruiser fast approaching. It was only when it revved its engine loudly that it stole Teresa's attention to what was behind.

"Fuck!" she screamed as she stamped on the gas pedal, the taxi speeding forward as fast as it could in its handicapped state.

But it could not travel for that much longer, as the rims were slowly starting to buckle inward, and soon, the whole side of the chassis would be touching the street.

The police cruiser was almost touching the cab's rear bumper as Teresa yanked at the wheel, making the car smash its way onto the sidewalk, taking out a parking meter and trash can beneath it.

Susan was thrown around like a doll as she desperately tried to grab onto something to steady her. She wanted to scream *stop* at Teresa but had noticed the police cruiser too and realized that they had to get away as fast as they could.

But the wheel's rims began to buckle under the car's weight, and the side of the cab suddenly dipped, catching on the pavement, yanking them to the left and sending them crashing into the back of a parked car.

Without pause and slightly dazed, Teresa turned

and grabbed her bag from the back seat. Quickly unzipping it, she pulled out her police issue revolver.

Susan, dazed and confused, was slumped across the seat, staring helplessly at Teresa.

"Get out, now," Teresa urged as she barged open the driver door with her shoulder, the frame having buckled outward in the collision.

As she got out to her feet, her gun aimed in her line of sight, Teresa looked behind her. The police cruiser was there. In the middle of the street. Engine off. Door open.

She knew better than to presume the car was empty, so she kept her aim on it as she looked around her surroundings. Looking for a moving shadow. Listening for the smallest of sounds. She was scared, but her training had kicked in. She had the gun. She was not going to be surprised by anything.

Susan, meanwhile, struggled as she stumbled out of the car, worse for wear from being tossed around in the getaway.

"You keep moving," Teresa said, not taking her eyes off her surroundings. "Take the next right, back to where the people are."

"I can't leave you," Susan replied.

"If you're not here, you've got more of a chance. If anything happens to me, you can be alive to tell people what happened, okay?" She turned with a no-nonsense look. "Now, go!"

Not arguing any more, Susan hurriedly walked on

in the direction they had been driving, a street that raised up a hill. Pushing herself, she ran as fast as she could, only occasionally looking back to Teresa, who remained aiming her gun around, vigilantly on the lookout for the pursuer.

Getting to the top of the hill, Susan could see across several blocks ahead. Streetlamp-lit, empty streets. Lined with closed stores, parked cars, and more warehouses. It was a dead part of town at this hour. Not even the junkies or hustlers came here.

Looking back over her shoulder, she could only see Teresa, the taxi cab, and the police cruiser. No maniac cop. No pursuer.

Walking over the apex of the hill, Susan kept to the sidewalk as she walked down a steep incline. Keeping close to the cars, she locked her gaze on every darkened doorway that she passed.

As her pace increased, she gained some confidence. Still keeping her back to the parked cars, she did not let a shadow pass without her checking within each one. She may not have been a beat cop, but she knew the dangers of taking your attention away from the darkness. For in there lay anything.

As she passed a group of parked cars, she did not notice that one of them, a battered old Chevrolet, had all of its windows smashed open. She just hurried by, keeping her eyes on the other side of the sidewalk.

A huge white-gloved hand reached out from within the Chevrolet, seizing her by the wrist. The hand was like a vise as it clamped down and dragged her nearer to the car. As it did, another gloved hand shot out, holding a pair of handcuffs. As one was slapped on her wrist, the metal clunked off the bone.

Susan let out a pained cry.

She tried to pull away, but the other end on the handcuff had been attached to the outside door handle.

She screamed louder as she tried to pull the cuffs off, wrenching against it and crying out for help.

Then the driver's side door opened, and *he* stepped out. Matthew Cordell.

As his monstrously large frame approached her, she went to scream louder, but the wind was suddenly knocked out of her as he grabbed around her waist and lifted her. His huge arm squashing any breath from her lungs.

As he pushed her into the open window of the cruiser, the man's smell hit her. The foulness made her gag and almost vomit down his mold-covered jacket.

Bang!

A shot rang out.

The bullet tore through the air and hit Cordell in the side of the head. A perfect kill shot.

But like all the other shots Teresa had fired into him, this one did as much damage.

Teresa raced down the hill, gun outward, knowing that shot would not kill him. She hoped that the bullets she did fire may at least slow the Maniac Cop down enough so that they could escape. But all her shots did, was alert him.

He let go of Susan and turned to face Teresa.

"Susan, run!" Teresa shouted as she got nearer and shot Cordell square in the chest.

"I can't," Susan yelped as she tried once more to pull her hand free of the cuffs.

Teresa marched toward Cordell with gritted teeth, emptying her last four shots into his face and heart. Hoping he would at least stumble.

He did not.

He just lunged at her, grabbing Teresa by the face. With horrifying strength, he lifted her off the ground and hurled her through the air. Her body flew across the sidewalk before smashing through a plate-glass window of Ozzie's Hardware Surplus. The impact instantly triggering the loud wail of the store's burglar alarm.

Cordell then turned to Susan, who still was frantically pulling at her handcuffs, hoping the old Chevy's handle would snap off. But she was not so lucky.

Instead of walking to her, Cordell went back around to the driver's side, reached into the broken window, released the hand brake, and threw the gear into drive.

Susan tried to get her footing as the car started to move sideways. As she tried to pull on the cuffs, she realized what the huge cop was doing. Using all of his strength, he was pulling the car away from the curb by gripping the door and roof through the window. With the brakes off and the car in drive, when out of the way of the other parked cars, the Chevy would not stay still. With the long incline ahead of it, it would roll. Roll fast.

"No, don't. *Don't*, please," Susan screamed, yanking at the cuffs desperately, ineffectually.

Her cries though fell on uncaring ears as Cordell just stepped back then gave the Chevy a strong shove. Instantly, the car began to roll forward and continue moving on its own momentum, with Susan moving tethered to it.

With over three hundred yards of a straight, empty sloping street ahead of them, the car had a long way to travel and a lot of speed to pick up.

Susan had to quicken her pace to avoid being dragged. She had to start running just to keep up with the Chevy.

Chained to this car, with her unsteady pace, Susan felt as if she would fall at any moment, and if she did, she would be pulled along the street. Along the unforgiving concrete.

She had to think fast and ignore the screaming in her brain, yelling at her that this was the end.

Back up the hill, the Maniac Cop watched the vehicle freewheel away at speed. He did not smile. He did not show any emotion. His heavily scarred and mutilated face did little apart from watching the event silently.

Running beside the Chevy, faster and faster, nearly at the maximum speed she could run, Susan had only one shot to not fall. She had to leap into the window of the door she had been cuffed to.

"Fuck, fuck, fuck, fuck, fuck," she spluttered in a panic as she built up the nerve to just go for it. With one hand on the inside of the window, she ignored the small jagged edge of the glass that cut into her palm. She threw herself inside the window, headfirst.

With one arm through and the other twisting at the wrist, still handcuffed to the outside of the door, her feet left the ground and started kicking in the air wildly, trying to move herself farther inside. She had to somehow get to the brake pedal. To stop the car from crashing. Whatever it may hit at this speed would be catastrophic for her. *She had to get to the brake and had to get to it now!*

With no driver at the wheel as well as the ignition off. The car had no control as it continued barreling down the hill. Slowly veering to the left where, up ahead, the street started to level out and a large truck was parked in the way.

She tried hard to wiggle through the window, but her cuffed wrist held her back. Reaching forward with her free hand, she did her best to avoid touching the wheel, and not wanting to veer the car into greater danger, instead, grabbed the edge of the dashboard, then pulled. Pulled as hard inward as she could.

As her body came in more, she started to fall down

onto the seat. In her panic, with her adrenaline pumping she did not feel the pressure on her wrist as her body moved further in the car. It was only when a loud crack sounded and a searing pain tore through all of her nerves that Susan realized her wrist had snapped under the twisting of the handcuffs.

Despite this, her body was fully inside the speeding Chevy, though her snapped wrist was still cuffed to the door, her hand lolling loosely against the air.

Moving her legs around as the pain from her broken bone made her scream in agony, she shoved her foot down under the steering wheel, into the driver's footwell. The brake pedal felt like a rock as without the vacuum assist of the engine, she didn't have the strength in her body to stop this car. If she was properly in the seat or she wasn't in such awful agony, it may have been different. But the car was still careening downward toward the parked truck.

She could only do one thing, grab the wheel with her good hand, but without the power steering, she could barely steer. Her other arm, twisted and still cuffed, shot bolts of searing pain into her brain as she yanked the wheel as hard as she could.

Managing to turn it a few degrees, the car narrowly avoided the truck and jumped up on the sidewalk, narrowly missing a lamppost as it grazed along a brick building on the other side. Like a pinball machine, the car ricocheted off the wall and sped back down over the curb and toward the intersection that lay ahead. An intersection where some traffic was passing by.

With the Chevy careening into a three-hundred-sixty-degree spin, it shot out across the junction and slammed into two cars that were traveling in opposite directions.

The deafening collision threw the Chevy into a roll. Susan was thrown about inside, slamming into surface, until they came to a violent stop, colliding against a line of stone bollards.

As the car jolted to a stop, she was thrown, tethered by her wrist, against the windshield, where she immediately lost consciousness as her head collided with the cracked glass.

In the ruins of Ozzie's Hardware Surplus' frontage, Teresa lay just inside on a bed of broken glass and broken display items. Her body was covered in lacerations from smashing through the window. She was bloody yet still conscious. Strong enough to stagger to her feet.

She immediately looked around for some kind of weapon. Her gun was useless—not that it had any use against Cordell when it had a bullet. She needed something she could use. Something more final.

Then she saw it.

Against the wall, fallen from a broken shelving unit, was a large chainsaw. A beastly looking tool that would definitely do a lot more damage than a bullet ever could.

Grabbing the saw's handle, she quickly grabbed its pull cord with her other hand and prayed hard. *Please, God, let there be fuel in this thing*, she begged.

The machine suddenly jerked into operation on its first pull. This chainsaw had been fully fueled due to some miracle. As its blade spun madly around, the scream from the motor only spurred her on. Her eyes were glazed yet determined. She promised herself. *I will finish this*.

Walking out of the store, she immediately saw Cordell standing there, looking away from her. Staring down the hill at the crash. He must have heard the saw, but he seemed not to care. He just looked at the smashed Chevy.

Teresa wasn't going to wait around to find out what was going on. She immediately rushed toward the Maniac Cop and thrust the chainsaw blade into his back.

Effortlessly the spinning teeth of the saw cut through the uniform and into his flesh and bone. She pushed the blade as hard as she could until it burst out of his stomach.

The wound did not spray any blood but just made a hole.

As if forcing him into paying attention, Cordell turned with a look of fury as he seized the rotating blade with one hand and snapped the end of it off, splitting the chain and rendering the saw powerless. The motor whined as it tried to spin the chain around, but nothing happened. It no longer had anything to turn.

Teresa immediately backed away, intending to rush back into the store and find another weapon. But Cordell was too fast. In one movement, he reached back and pulled the chainsaw from his back, dropping it to the ground, then reached out and grabbed her.

She screamed in terror as Cordell pulled her toward him, spinning her around into his waiting embrace. Nothing she could do could stop this cop from lifting her up as both of his arms wrapped around her waist and then started to squeeze.

As her ribs snapped inward with a series of loud cracks, their sharp, splintered ends sliced through the delicate tissue of her lungs. The once rhythmic rise and fall of her chest was obliterated in an instant, replaced by the wet, hollow sound of air escaping into her organs. His arms compressed harder and harder as she desperately screamed.

Inside the wreckage of the runaway vehicle, Susan was straddling consciousness. Her eyes were unable to focus, the pain in her wrist was evenly matched with the pain in her head. A large gash across the top of her forehead seeped out blood that coated her face as she tried to stay awake.

Through her blurry vision, she could see the head-lights of a car pull up and the unmistakable shape of a cop standing there and watching her for a moment, then crouch and reach inside.

She screamed and struggled against this figure as a silhouette of a second cop appeared in the lights and joined with the first, reaching in toward her.

They came into focus. Their silhouettes breaking and the detail of their NYPD uniforms and young faces coming into view.

"She's handcuffed?" one of the cops said in surprise.

The second cop stared at her "Lady, can you hear me? Who cuffed you? Lady? *Lady*?"

The first soon noticed the police badge clipped to her belt. "Shit, she's one of ours."

Susan, meanwhile, could not stop struggling and trying to scream in her weakened and delirious state.

"Easy does it," the second cop said to her. "We'll get you out of here."

Both figures stood and became silhouettes in the headlights once more. She could hear what they were saying, even if, in her state, she could not understand what the words meant.

"Radio in and get help up here. We gotta get her out."

Susan then lost consciousness. She did not wake as the handcuffs were unlocked to free her snapped wrist or when an emergency responder used a hydraulic rescue tool, the jaws of life, to wrench the Chevy's door off its hinges to get her out of the wreck.

It was only when she was strapped onto a gurney and placed inside the ambulance that she started to come to. And as she did, the knowledge of what she had seen quickly overtook her.

"She shot him," she slurred weakly. "Six times . . . He didn't die. Didn't even bleed."

"Lie still," the paramedic urged as he was taping up her wrist with a splint.

"Please . . . I have to go." She tried to keep her focus as she spoke. "Teresa . . . She's still up there."

From outside, she noticed a familiar face. Detective Lieutenant McKinney. He stood, staring in at her, with a troubled look.

"McKinney . . . I saw him," Susan said in a whimper. "I saw what he can do . . . Cordell."

McKinney shook his head. He did not know what to say. He has just come from where Teresa was lying on the floor, blood spewing from her mouth, her chest crushed and her neck snapped. Twisted around one-hundred-eighty degrees. Somehow, she was still grasping to her life. Her body was contorted in so many ways. Arms, fingers, and legs all splayed out in different directions.

As she was loaded into an ambulance, the paramedics doubted she could survive. It was plain to see that whatever had gotten to her was a thing of immense strength, brutality, and cruelty, but McKinney could still not believe it was Matthew Cordell who did the deed. He had no doubt it was the same Maniac Cop from eighteen months ago. But he did not think for one moment that it was who Susan believed it was.

"He was shot in the head," Susan continued. Struggling for her voice to be heard as she balanced on the precipice of consciousness. "He was dead . . . He kept on coming. *He was dead*!"

Chapter 5

Criminals At Large was a divisive news show. Filmed live with a studio audience, it was the brainchild of the presenter Donnie Johns and was a low brow, sensationalistic tabloid cable show and one of the most popular in New York City. One that relished shocks over facts and one that allowed anyone on it as long as they had a story to tell that could rile up their fanbase. For every real criminal they reported on, another dozen were purely fictitious, with facts taking a backseat to supposition and fear. An old woman who fell down the stairs and died would not be reported. But two happening in the same week in the same city? That was a serial killer, according to Donnie Johns. *The Staircase Slayer*, as he dubbed it. After that every fall was caused by this invented assassin. And so many people actually believed it—so many that City Hall could not ignore the impact and reach the show had, even though it wanted to pretend the show didn't exist. The people believed the show to the point that they bought the merch, watched every show, became part of Donnie's cult of personality. Not that he had much of a real personality. And on the streets, you would often see someone wearing one of the many T-shirts. It may have been trash TV but was trash that officials had to often appear on, to try and quell the lies about certain cases.

"Tonight," Donnie Johns announced to the camera, sat in a high-backed swivel chair. "*Criminals At Large* goes after a serial killer who has claimed the lives of beautiful young women across New York City, exotic dancers. And you, the audience, can help us catch this beast."

The glare of the studio lights shone down on his orange perma tan. With an obvious wig and shining veneers, he was a caricature of a presenter and every bit as much of a low-rent muck-raker as even the most unethical journalist. But his show was so popular. People across the city sat glued to each broadcast to see what would happen live, and every week, there would be something new unearthed that would be the talk of all watercooler meetings the following day. And during these live studio recordings, the audience lapped it up in an almost bloodthirsty passion with jeers, cheers, and whoops.

Donnie continued his introduction. "They are the victims. Tonight, you'll meet detectives assigned to this case. You'll meet friends of the victims, but first, here is the man in charge of it all, Commissioner Edward Doyle."

The camera pulled back to reveal the commissioner sitting in a smaller chair next to Donnie. He looked very uncomfortable at having to be here. Forced into it by the mayor, he could not hide the look of disdain from his face.

Donnie smiled. "Tell us how the department is handling this case, Commissioner."

Doyle took a deep breath in before replying in a monotone. "We've assembled a task force to handle the investigation, but in addition, we've had officers alert all the young women who are part of the suspect's target group. Telling them of the dangers and to be extra vigilant."

Hearing something on his hidden earpiece, Donnie's expression turned quizzical as he looked to the audience, and saw Susan Riley, her lower arm plastered with a bandage over the top half of her head. She was being helped down the aisle by a production assistant. Each step making her wince as she was led to the microphone at the front of the crown. One which was used for any audience Q&As.

"Sorry for a break in the schedule so far, but I've just been informed that we have someone here who can shed some light on this as a counter to what you said, Commissioner. We'll hear from a police psychologist no less. Let's see what Susan Riley has to say."

As the audience gave a polite round of applause,

Doyle looked shocked at Susan being there. He had been told of what had happened and her terrible injuries, but he never expected she would be walking around, let alone here now.

When she spoke, Susans's voice was weak yet determined. "The murders of these exotic dancers is a tragic situation, but it's a matter of public record. Everything about the investigation has already been reported. There's another series of killings going on in the city that's being covered up by the commissioner and everyone higher up in the NYPD."

Donnie was ecstatic at hearing this, but on the outside, he just looked studious as he nodded. "Commissioner, your thoughts on this accusation?"

Doyle waved his hand at Riley dismissively. "This is nonsense," he grumbled. "This isn't the case I am here to discuss."

Susan continued. "The Maniac Cop did not drown in the river as reported." She ignored the soreness over her body, the pain in her wrist. She wanted to be lucid and had not taken the prescribed painkillers yet. "He's has killed three times again."

People in the audience audibly gasped.

"Commissioner?" Donnie prompted.

Doyle shook his head. He wanted to get out of there. "The homicides of which Officer Riley is speaking were deliberately set up to imitate the earlier killings. It's a sensitive case, which we will inform the public of at a relevant stage, but now . . . It is not the time or place for any ludicrous proclamations."

Donnie's eyes showed his delight, even if his expression didn't. "So, you're saying the Maniac Cop isn't back and someone is dressing up and copying the MO of that killer?"

Doyle didn't reply.

"Then, if that's the case, why has it been kept from the public?" Susan asked pointedly. "They have a right to know. What are you hiding?"

Losing his temper, Doyle raised his voice. "The killer craves publicity. When we don't give it to him, we expect him to be foolhardy, to *show* himself, and that's when we nail him. If everyone knows he's out there, he'll become more careful." He then stood from the chair and turned to Susan angrily. "I do want to say we were *very* close to making an arrest."

"Commissioner Doyle"—she smiled as she spoke— "why don't you admit . . . it's Officer Matthew Cordell who's responsible?"

"*No!* He's dead," Doyle bellowed. "He died in prison."

"Officer Teresa Mallory is in a coma, not expected to survive because she knew it was Matthew Cordell, and he came after her. She was—*is*—a brave, brave woman who had discovered that he did not die years ago as the commissioner wants you to think. Instead, he was brain-dead but still breathing when his body was released. She was going to come here tonight to tell everyone what she knew. But as she can't, I am."

"See? You just admitted it. He was brain-dead?!" Doyle said, turning to Donnie. "He can't be a killer."

"Did you just admit that this Cordell didn't die as you just said a few moments ago?" Doyle asked, a smile creeping over his face, catching the commissioner in his contradictory words.

"N-No," Doyle said in sudden shock. "I just meant . . ."

Susan continued, speaking over the commissioner. "Cordell recovered and came back to avenge himself on the police department and the city officials who railroaded him into jail. Who used him as a scapegoat. Commissioner Doyle insists on hiding these facts! Why?"

Across Manhattan, in the Pink Pussy Club, a neon, seedy dive of a strip joint, a handful of male patrons were sitting at shadowed tables around a podium placed in the center of the room. Upon which, three tired, topless dancers gyrated. Each looked disinterested and moved in a halfhearted way. The patrons didn't mind, though. They just wanted to see bare flesh. They didn't care how it moved as long as it moved.

At the bar, a man in his thirties was sat. Stephen Turkell. He was not watching the naked women.

Instead, his eyes fixated on the small television behind the bar. *Criminals At Large* was playing live. The sound, while low, was still audible despite the background music.

This man, with a mess of long brown hair, stared at the screen with his pale eyes, not blinking. His bushy beard framed his chapped lips that barely covered a mess of brown, rotten teeth. This man carried with him a constant unhinged expression.

On the screen, Donnie Johns had just thanked Susan Riley and addressed the audience. "Criminals At Large intends to investigate these allegations about the identity of the Maniac Cop in full, and we will have an explosive report on it next week. But we'll now resume our investigation of the murder of the exotic dancers in midtown New York."

In the studio, Donnie continued to speak to the camera, signing off for an advert break as offscreen, Doyle tore off his microphone. The commissioner then rushed across the studio to confront Susan, who was about to leave, propped up by the production assistant.

"You stupid little bitch!" he seethed through gritted teeth. "I'm going to see that you're suspended, and that's a fact."

Susan did not rise to any of this man's bluster. "Teresa Mallory is lying on a bed in the hospital, with tubes coming out of her, barely alive, because she knew the *truth*, and you did nothing. *That* is the fact here. And Cordell will most likely pay you a visit, too. You know that, right? You are part of this. You'll see him, just like I did. And you'll wish you did something about it sooner."

Turning, Susan hobbled back up the steps, shooing away the production assistant. She may have been injured, but she managed walking away by herself.

Doyle glared after her. After she left, he turned and saw Donnie Johns speaking to an assistant.

"Get everything you can on this Officer Matthew Cordell. I don't care how you do it, just get it before the *Post* runs with it."

Doyle sighed. The cat was well and truly out of the bag, and Cordell's name was going to be on everyone's lips.

At the Pink Pussy Club, Turkell still stared at the show on the television as its credits rolled.

"Now we've got a newcomer," the slimy emcee said on the mic from his place in the DJ booth.

Catching Turkell's attention, he turned back to the stage to see who this new dancer was.

The emcee continued. "The winner of Monday night's topless contest. Please put your Pink Pussy hands together and welcome the lovely, the seductive, the innocent, the erotic . . . Miss Lenore."

A young and somewhat awkward nineteen-year-old woman appeared on stage, dressed in a gold tasseled bra and panties, complete with matching stilettos. She quickly began her dance as the beat to her song kicked in.

It was obvious that she was not experienced in doing this. She was visibly nervous and not at all like the other bored dancers, who had plied their trades here every night. She was just a kid. Her name obviously wasn't Miss Lenore; it was Cheryl Dandridge. She stepped off the bus from Oakville, Ohio, less than two years ago. She had never planned on doing this, but with her savings nearly gone and rent becoming a struggle, she was out of options. She had worked as a barmaid in various strip clubs across the city, including this one until tonight, but the pay was too low, and shifts were becoming scarce. The dancers she met in the clubs often told her she was lucky, both pretty and pert, which meant she could make a lot of money with minimal effort.

So, she entered the topless competition here to see if she could even do that. To her surprise, she won twenty dollars and was immediately offered a dancing position. So, she made herself get the nerve. And here she was, trying to not succumb to those nerves.

The sparse crowd of the club perked up as they paid more attention to a new flesh on show. Seated at the bar, Turkell fixated on her. Wide-eyed, intense, unsettling. His gaze never wavered, tracking each hesitant movement she made. To her, she felt unsure, awkward. But to him, she exuded confidence and allure.

Off the Great White Way, past the bright lights and blinking theater district marquees, sat West 42nd Street. A hub for sex shows, dealers, pimps, hustlers, and low-rent hotels. It was not a safe neighborhood by any means but was one that some had no choice but to stay in.

In one of the many flea-ridden hotels, The DeWitt, rooms were rented by the hour, day, week or month. A favorite spot for sex workers who could not afford apartments. It was a hotel that may not have been nice to look at but at least it was dry—aside from the leaks in some rooms—and warm when the heating bothered to work.

Up on the fourth floor of the DeWitt, in room 404, Cheryl Dandridge had made a home.

Her tiny room was decorated as best as she could afford. All the furniture had been provided by the hotel but could only be considered threadbare at best. There was a smattering of plump cushions upon them, pictures on the wall, throws, and rugs masking the true state of what they had been thrown over.

Upon an old stained and cracked mirror on the wall, a handful of photographs had been stuck. Ones that covered up the breaks but also reminding Cheryl of who she once was before she came here. Images taken many years ago, ones where she was a ballerina back in Oakville. A dancer with dreams of making it big in the Big Apple.

On the dresser table in front of the mirror, a copy of *Variety* lay open, and underneath that lay torn out job sections from local newspapers. Each page covered in crossings out and circles. Mapping the jobs applied for.

With her gold tasseled bra and panties thrown in a heap on the floor, Cheryl was freshly showered and slightly damp as she sat huddled on the sofa in her dressing gown. She was talking on the telephone.

"Sure, there's good opportunities for advancement," she said into the receiver. Her voice quiet. "There's also an employee cafeteria, so I'm getting plenty to eat." The lies she told her mother had become commonplace. Thankfully, her folks would never be able to visit the city to find out the truth, with money worries and their medical needs. They never went anywhere. As for the time of this call, Cheryl mother was like she was, a night owl. So, a call at 2 a.m. was usual and weekly.

Cheryl continued her fictional tale. "I'm sharing this nice apartment with a couple of the girls in the secretarial pool. So, don't worry. I just needed that money for a deposit. I've got food and all nice stuff."

Her mother was not stupid, though, and could tell from her daughter's voice that all was not as it seemed.

But as long as she got her call every week, she would not worry too much.

"Give my love to Dad, okay?" Cheryl said, signing off. "I love you so much . . . Bye."

Hanging up the phone, Cheryl sluggishly moved off the sofa, taking the phone with her and put it back on the dresser. As she did, she caught sight of herself in the mirror. With her garish makeup washed off and the baby oil no longer on her body to make it glisten under the spotlight, Cheryl felt shame. She hated lying to her mother, but what was the alternative? *Oh, hi, Mom, I'm fine. I'm just stripping for a bunch of perverts across town. No, don't worry, I have enough money to barely make ends meet. I may even have to become a hooker soon just so that I can afford food. Now, how's Dad doing?*

"Yeah, Mom," she muttered as she stared at herself. "My typing's getting *much* better." With a sigh, she turned to make her way to her bed, when a noise made her pause.

Something at the door . . . a light jiggling of the doorknob.

Slowly stepping over, Cheryl looked alert and worried. She may be new to the city, but she had seen enough to know to not trust anyone or anything. Ever. Though it was probably only a drunk unable to find their own room, she didn't discount anything more sinister. Not in this part of the city.

"Who is it?" she called out. "I know someone's

there!" She paused for a beat but heard no reply. "I got a gun, you know? And I'm not afraid to use it!" She did not have a gun, and she was terrified at the very thought of them.

Slowly, she leaned nearer to the peep hole in the door.

Staring out, the fish-eye lens showed only an empty corridor outside, complete with a flickering lightbulb on the ceiling that hadn't been fixed since she arrived here ten months ago.

But there was something. It wasn't totally empty. Through the hole, there was . . . something. At the bottom of her vision was the edge of a blur on the rim of the lens. Like something just out of view. Hiding.

Looking down, where the light would normally break through the gap at the bottom of the door and spill in over the stained carpeting, was a solid shadow.

Someone was out there, hiding just below the vision of the peephole.

Getting brave, Cheryl kicked at the bottom of the door hard. Trying to scare away whatever was out there.

Her kick quickly provoked whatever had been lurking on the outside, forcing it to move away in a fury. The light beneath the door reappeared as the shadow darted. Moments later, the door began to tremble under the force of a heavy pounding, the lock rattling with each blow.

Someone wanted in.

Not wanting to wait, Cheryl rushed for the phone, nervously picked it up, and dialed the operator.

Down in the lobby, the tired and bored desk clerk lazily picked up the call.

"Front desk," he lazily said.

"This is 404. Someone's trying to break into my room."

"That's impossible! Nobody came up there," the clerk replied. Barely showing a glint of care.

"I'm telling you, he's out there. Can't you hear him?"

Even over the phone, the pounding on the door was loud and clear.

"Maybe a guest got the wrong room by mistake?"

"Call the goddamn cops!" Cheryl pleaded.

The clerk rolled his eyes at the receiver. "We don't want cops here . . . Just ignore it."

The pounding on the door continued in the background as Cheryl's voice grew more frantic.

"Call them or give me a line. I'll do it myself!"

The clerk sighed. "Fine. Have it your way. But if I were in your line of work, the last people I'd wanna see are the cops."

"What the hell do you mean? What kind of fucking remark is that?"

"I'll call 'em, okay?" the clerk said without care as he then clicked off the line.

Slowly, the clerk then dialed 911. He waited for the call to connect. His eyes gazed around the dank reception room. It was too late for this, but he was too disinterested to talk about it more. This would be all he would do. He would waste everyone's time.

The call connected.

"Emergency services, how may I direct your call."

"Police," he lazily uttered.

Cheryl, offended by the call and scared by the incessant pounding at her door, hung up the phone. Looking around, she tried to find any object she may be able to use as a weapon.

Picking up the heaviest thing she could lay her hands on, an old metal lamp, she quickly pulled its power cord out from the wall socket, sending the room into a sudden darkness.

Almost on cue, the pounding on the door stopped as if the power had been cut to that, too. And as it did, Cheryl's heartbeat sped up.

Maybe he's gone, she thought.

"I called the cops," she said nervously. "They're coming. You better get out of here, right now."

There was no response. There was no sound at all.

She stared at her front door in silent prayer, slowly backing away from it. Relief soon began to set in as she placed the lamp back on the dresser.

Shaking off her negative feeling, she couldn't help

but let out a small chuckle. Bending down to plug the light back in, she could not help but resent the fact that she would need to call the desk clerk up again. Apologize and admit he was right. It *must* have just been some drunk guy coming home from a night out, who was—

As she was in mid-thought, the window leading to the fire escape smashed inward as a dark figure came hurtling through it.

Before she could get away or scream, the thickly built figure had knocked her to the floor, pinning her down on her well-worn carpet. It was a man with the wild, unblinking stare of a psychopath. It was Stephen Turkell. He leered closer, his grin stretched unnaturally wide, exposing his jagged set of brown teeth, ruined, rotting stumps, looking like a decaying Cheshire Cat. A stench of decay mixed with terrible halitosis seeped from his infected gums as he breathed over her. A putrid cocktail of an odor that rolled over her in waves. It invaded her nostrils, turning her stomach inside out. She gagged violently as her body tried to recoil, but he was too strong.

"I've been watching you," Turkell said lasciviously as a string of drool dripped over his cracked lips and down onto her cheek. "I watched you dance . . . You've been asking for this."

Around his neck hung a small Polaroid camera. With one hand, he pushed her down, and with the other, he grabbed his camera, held it up, and snapped a picture. A picture of Cheryl fighting for her life. The camera flashed brightly as the photo reeled out of the cartridge. Grabbing the photo without waiting for it to develop, he stuffed it into his pocket with a grin and let go of the camera.

"I called the police!" Cheryl cried out in panic as she tried to writhe free.

"Oh no," he replied, his face looking genuinely concerned. "Don't worry. It'll all be okay. This won't take long. I promise. I'll be gone soon enough." Turkell then just smiled wider as he stared at her, gripping her harder as she continued to struggle.

"You're him, aren't you?" she asked weakly, her eyes filling with tears as she realized what this was. "You killed those girls."

"I like photos, you see?" he said, his voice almost childlike. "I've got a great collection. But you'll be the prettiest, and you dance better than the others. Good enough to be on Broadway!"

Desperate, she said, "I got auditions to do some musicals!"

She had no idea why she said that. She didn't have any auditions. She couldn't even get that far in the process. She was just trying anything to change the focus.

"Oh yeah?" He beamed. "That's great." His smile then dropped to a sneer. "Much better than being up on that jizz-soaked bar, shaking your cunt for the world to see. Pity you'll never make those auditions now."

At that moment, Turkell's disgusting words were interrupted by the sharp ring of the telephone.

"That's them," Cheryl said. "They're down in the lobby. They're gonna come up and catch you. You should run!" She tried pleading with him, making him think she was on his side, but he was deaf to her words.

"I figure I've got at least a minute," he grinned as she felt a hard, fleshy object pushing against her thigh. "And that's more than enough time for this."

He slipped his hands around her throat, and as he did, he could not help but giggle playfully.

As she fought back, he started singing to himself. "Amazing grace, how sweet the sound. That saved a wretch like me." His hands squeezed tighter as his off-key singing made this whole experience so much more terrifying. "I once was lost, but now I'm found. Was blind, but now I see."

Grabbing his hands with hers, Cheryl dug her nails into his flesh, breaking the skin with ease. But instead of screaming and pulling away, the moan he let out was something more twisted. His grip tightened even more.

"Thank you," he whispered before carrying on his song. "'Twas grace that taught my heart to fear. And grace my fear—"

A sudden banging on the door made the strangled Cheryl smile. *They are here to save me*, she thought.

Turkell looked up incensed. He wanted more time. He *needed* more time.

All at once, the sound of smashing wood filled the

room as the apartment door broke into multiple pieces, flying off its hinges as a silhouette of a giant policeman stood in the corridor.

It was the Maniac Cop, Matthew Cordell. Swiftly, he strode into the room.

Turkell immediately lost all bravado as he scurried backward, releasing Cheryl from his grip. He pulled a knife out from his jacket pocket, and held it up defensively.

Cheryl stared up at the cop, barely able to breathe as she mouthed the words *Thank you.*

But Cordell reached down, grabbed her by the neck again, and lifted her from the ground. Taking over from Turkell's throttling. Her feet dangled in the air as she tried to kick away. She screamed as much as she could in his grip. Her eyes filling with a renewed feral panic.

Turkell meanwhile, stared at this brutality in awe. The cop didn't come after him. He came for *her*. As he stared, he felt his trousers get even tighter as he watched the life being strangled out of his victim.

Through the reception area of The DeWitt Hotel, two uniformed police officers ran toward the staircase. Following them, the desk clerk looked panicked.

When they had arrived outside the hotel a couple of minutes ago, the police had witnessed Turkell smash in through an upstairs apartment window. Room 404.

They hurried up the flights of stairs with ease as the desk clerk wheezed behind them, lagging further and further behind with exhaustion.

Getting to the fourth-floor landing, the police raced down the corridor, where the front door to room 404 had been smashed in.

Turning into the apartment, neither officer had time to speak or draw their weapons as Cheryl's limp body flew through the air toward them. Slamming into them, sending them to the carpet with a thud.

The Maniac Cop had thrown her as he grabbed the billy club from his belt. Almost casually, he twirled it around his wrist by the strap. The club spun around with speed, where he caught it firmly on the other side. Then he twisted the club and revealed the hidden, long stiletto blade.

The cops, dazed, struggled to get to their feet as they went for their guns, but Cordell was too fast upon them.

He plunged his blade into one of the cop's temples, killing him instantly. Cordell did not stop with him as his other hand started repeatedly punching the man in his face, holding his limp body up by the embedded blade. Punch after punch after punch, the rage in this maniac cop was feral. His last punch landed on the officer's face so hard the stiletto blade was forced out from the officer's temple to the front of his face.

The other officer stared in shock as his eyes then fell to Turkell, who had his hands down his trousers, frantically masturbating as he watched the violence ecstatically.

Cheryl, her neck badly bruised and swelling, was grasping onto life. Staring up at her real rescuers, being murdered by this . . . *thing*. She couldn't understand the damage on Cordell's face as she stared up at him. The mass of deep gouges. The hole where his nose once was. His one sunken eye and other bulging one. His deathly pallor.

As the stiletto blade left the murdered officer's skull, his body was hurled forward by Cordell. The body went flying out of the room and into the corridor, slamming into the wall before landing in a bloody heap on the floor.

Outside, the approaching desk clerk was out of breath but finally at the fourth floor. He saw the officer's body and screamed, running back down the staircase.

The second cop inside the room tried to run but was grabbed and tossed against the dresser. Gripping this man by the hair on the back of his head, Cordell smashed him hard into the mirror opposite. The force was so immense that the policeman's skull cracked open wide with one hit. And as it did, Cheryl's photos fell down onto the carpet with broken shards of mirror, blood, and brain matter.

In one motion, Cordell dropped the man to the floor, resheathed his stiletto blade, then attached it to his belt. He then turned on Turkell, who was still in mid-stroke. Walking over, he grabbed him by the arm, then dragged him toward the window and out onto the fire escape. Turkell finishing in his trousers as he did.

The distant sound of police sirens could be heard in the distance as Cordell pulled him down the metal steps. All the while, Turkell was staring up at Cordell as if he were his savior, and after what just happened, he was.

As they reached street level. Cordell let go and started to walk away, down a dark alley by The DeWitt, toward the street beyond.

Pausing for a moment in shock at what happened, Turkell finally pulled his other hand out of his pants, wiped it sloppily on his jacket, and trailed after the Maniac Cop.

"You saved me? You can't be a cop, can you . . ." The words from his mouth quickly faded as he realized who this horrific goliath was. Remembering what happened eighteen months ago and from the *Criminals at Large* show. Giddy excitement flooded from his mouth. "Wait! I know you! She was talking about you. The broad on the television. You're *him*!"

Cordell slowed down to a stop. The alley was so dark Turkell could not see anything except the Maniac Cop's colossal shape.

Moving closer, he smiled and chuckled. Reaching out, he put his hand on Cordell's arm. "You're my brother. You get that?" he said happily. "You and me, we're the same. We're victims. Victims of the world. Victims of our own rage. We are bonded."

Cordell didn't react. He just turned and stared at the small, filthy man.

Turkell continued. "But you're *so* much better than me. Front-page material. Whereas me? I'm back on page five . . . That's if I'm lucky. You get mayors, I get sluts . . . You see, no one is scared of me enough. You, though? The uniform. Your rage . . . *That* gets their attention. You are a god."

The Maniac Cop turned and started to walk away again.

Turkell's face fell. Feeling as if he was being shunned. So, he ran ahead and circled in front of Cordell, blocking his path. His words came out with desperation as he held his hands up to him, motioning to stop. "You don't wanna be out on the streets . . . It's crawling with cops around here . . . But I got a place. A quiet place. Real private . . . Come on . . . I wanna show you my collection . . ."

Cordell stared as Turkell started to walk away, beckoning him with his hand.

"Trust me," he called back. "We're friends. We're the same. I'll look out for you."

The sirens in the far streets were getting closer.

"We haven't got time!" Turkell urged. "You gotta come on!"

Chapter 6

In The DeWitt Hotel, a crime scene photographer was taking pictures of the two policemen's bodies. One was crumpled into a bloody heap in the corridor outside room 404. The other was inside the room, virtually headless, with its cranial remnants splattered all over the mirror and dresser.

Detective Lovejoy stood with his back to the gore, feeling sick as he always did. Sitting on the chair in front of him was Cheryl, alive and injured. As she breathed, the air came in a sore rasp as she forced herself to speak. Her head was pounding, and she felt like she could throw up at any given moment. The only thing stopping her was her need to stay alive and in the present. She had to focus herself to make sure she told them everything.

Lovejoy could not get over the smell of the room,

the acrid tang of both Turkell and Cordell's foulness. Both of their stinks as one created an even more pungent bouquet, which was hard to breathe. Lovejoy held his notepad in his hand and just directed his attention on the girl and her statement.

Cheryl croaked her words. "He admitted to me that he was the one who killed the other girls," she said.

"You mean the dead strippers?" he asked.

She glared. "I mean the *dancers*."

Lovejoy paused. "Right," he then replied. But still wrote down the word *strippers* into his notepad. "And there were two of them? Sheesh . . . I gotta say we didn't think of a pair doing this."

"No, they didn't know each other."

Lovejoy looked up from his notes. "But you said they took off together?"

Cheryl thought, replaying the moment the door burst open. "When I saw the bigger one come through the door, I was so relieved. I'd called down to the front desk for them to get the police. So, I thought he was there 'cause of me. But he was not. He was dressed as a cop. And the guy that killed the dancers, the one here first, he looked as scared as I was when that man came in." She paused for a second to swallow painfully. "But you know what, they didn't leave together, really. The cop dragged the other one out with him. Not really given him a chance." Thinking, she looked up at Lovejoy. "You think it could have been two killers crossing paths? I saw that in a movie once."

Lovejoy felt a chill. "If it was, you are damn, damn lucky."

Cheryl looked to the floor at her bare feet again. "Wonder how many people like that are running around the city," she mused hoarsely.

Lovejoy smiled, as this was a conversation he knew about. He knew stats. He knew *all* the crime stats. That was his passion. Not this. Not standing on a lump of brain, which, unbeknownst to him, he was.

"Our best estimate from recent analysis, and you can never be exact, is around twelve to fifteen serial killers, just in the New York and New Jersey areas alone. Maybe three hundred fifty of them running around the country as we speak. That's what the FBI says about it, anyway . . . So, I'm sure this is not unheard of, if they were both crossing paths, but it sure isn't usual."

"I guess either of them could come back to finish me off," she said, her voice getting weaker with each word. "He took my picture. He knows where I work."

Through the dark alleys and side streets, Turkell led the Maniac Cop further toward his lair, looking back at him every few seconds. Joyous that his new friend was here and following.

As Turkell reached the end of an alley, a long fence sat in their path. He was ready to climb over as he always did on this way home. He quickly gripped the cold chain-link fence, but before he could wrench himself over, a shadow loomed beside him.

Cordell, silently glared at the obstacle. Without a word, he raised his gloved hands and seized the chain links. A loud creak of bending metal filled the air around them as he pulled, his fingers wrenching the steel apart as if it were nothing more than paper mesh. The links soon broke apart under an immense force.

Turkell froze as he witnessed this. *That strength. It's not human. It can't be*, he thought.

Cordell then spread the torn metal wide, wordlessly inviting Turkell through the new gap.

Swallowing his awe but unable to silence a laugh, Turkell clambered through the metal hole. As soon as he was through, Cordell didn't hesitate. He seized the edges again and wrenched the hole even wider, the metal shrieking as he pulled a larger gap to fit himself through.

"You, my friend, are fucking *awesome*," Turkell said, slapping Cordell on the arm. Cordell, naturally, did not reply. He just looked blankly ahead.

Walking through a small discarded alley brimming with overgrown weeds, Turkell led them up to a hidden broken door. One that led into unused maintenance catwalks running underneath the Williamsburg Bridge.

"Just over here," Turkell said, pointing down the catwalk. "My place is just on the other side."

With the outline of the city visible through the slats on the metal walkways, they traversed slowly. Cordell's heavy boots thudding loudly with each step.

Now side by side, Turkell stared up at Cordell's face, admiring the mutilation. Finding him fascinating.

"You don't talk much, do you?" Turkell smiled. "That's okay. I can speak enough for both of us . . . Was it 'cause of an accident that you don't talk? Same one that did that to your face?"

Cordell looked down at Turkell as they walked, a question finally getting his attention. As he did, the city lights caught on the mauled remnants of his face, highlighting it.

"You're one beautiful bastard, you know that, right?" Turkell grinned. "Wish I looked like that."

Cordell looked back ahead, and they carried on walking.

"I can hide you. Keep you safe. Run errands. Whatever you need. We can look after each other. Two dicks are better than one, ya know what I mean?"

The rest of the journey carried on the same. Turkell babbling at speed as Cordell just walked beside him. Until, eventually, they reached the other side, where a large derelict building stood. Derelict aside from one apartment at the bottom. Turkell's home. With its own entrance at the back of the building, it was quite secluded and private.

"These are my girls," Turkell said as he walked

over to a cork board on the wall, where six other were pinned.

Each was a Polaroid of different women, each taken at the final moments of their lives. The fear on their faces through the lens was palpable. This was his rogue's gallery of victims.

He took out the Polaroid stuffed in his jacket pocket. Fully developed, the photograph showed Cheryl screaming into the camera as she lay on the floor of her apartment. The moment she faced her own death, caught in a single flash.

He pinned this up with a thumbtack, alongside the others.

They were both standing in Turkell's dingy basement apartment. A one room space with an old stained mattress in one corner and the remains of many meal trays stacked up in a filthy kitchenette sink.

Cordell stood at one end of the room. The darkest, most shadowed portion of it. His sheer size dwarfed this small place as he regarded Turkell in front of the photographs of his victims.

Turkell continued as he took the camera from around his neck and placed it on the sideboard. He spoke as he stared at the photos. "They'll never take their clothes off in front of anybody else again. They're Turkell's girls now. That's me, you see?" He turned to Cordell. "We never got a proper introduction. I'm Steve Turkell."

Cordell stood there, immobile as ever, almost like a piece of furniture. He stared at Turkell wherever he moved in the apartment. Tracing his steps. As if studying him.

Crossing to the kitchenette, Turkell grabbed a nearly empty bottle of whiskey from the side board. He poured what was left of the liquor between two unclean glasses. When done, he walked over to Cordell and held one of the glasses up to him.

After a few moments of nothing, Turkell shrugged. "Yeah, I took you for a clean kinda guy," he said, downing his own whiskey. "No worries. As I said, I'm here to help you. And I can help you with this," he then downed Cordell's measure. "I might as well tell you something about me, right? As we're getting to know each other." He returned the glasses to the sink, not to wash but where they would be until the next drink was bought. "Most of the time, I just talk to myself. Not like some of those guys who hear voices. I'm not like that . . . I mean, I don't hear no angels or devils telling me what to do. That's crazy. I *know* what to do. It's what I *want* to do." He grabbed a rickety chair, then sat. "Take a seat if you want? No need to stand." His offer was met with the expected response. "I *can* tell that you hate the police. So, you make a fucking mockery out of them," he laughed. "For a while, everybody was afraid to walk up to a cop in this town! You did that! Then they put out that you'd been killed. I didn't believe that for a second. You can't just kill people like us, but I gotta say, I never expected that we'd meet, that we'd become friends."

Cordell did not move or make a sound. Even his breathing was not audible. None of this deterred Turkell from carrying on his one-sided conversation.

"All right, let's get down to brass tacks . . . Why should you trust me?" he said. "I know I gotta earn that from you. I gotta show you that you can respect me. I gotta show you that I'm here for you. *With* you. Maybe you see possibilities in me, too? I hope so. I mean, why else would you be here?" He thought for a moment as he looked at the towering monster in front of him. A monster he saw as beautiful. "I get that you don't speak, but can you write? Can you write down your name so I know what to call you?"

A few seconds passed of silence. Then, suddenly, a low, rasping whisper filled the air, guttural and broken, forcing itself through shredded vocal cords, scraping like rusted metal. A word, just a single word, then spilled from the twisted, mangled lips of the Maniac Cop. Yet, despite his grotesque damage, the word was very clear.

"Cor . . . dell . . ."

And as he heard it, a chill ran through Turkell. A chill that made him stare up at the cop in total adoration. As if hearing the voice of God. His wide, rotten smile beamed as he nodded. "Cordell? Just like she said on the television? Well, Cordell, you are my hero."

. . .

The television screen was bright as the midday news report began. On the screen, the newscaster, Tom Shepard, spoke in grave and ominous tones. "New York City is once again reeling from what seems to be the presence of the Maniac Cop, back on our streets. The city is paralyzed with fear at the mounting rumors of a uniformed police officer prowling the streets, committing murder, striking down average citizens without provocation. I broke the story eighteen months ago about the Maniac Cop, and we thought it was over, especially after the NYPD *assured* us it was. But was that a coverup? Were those in power hiding their failures? Or is this a second murderer? Possibly, could this be the work of a coordinated cult? At this juncture, we just don't know. All we *do* know is that New York is in danger. We interviewed some citizens of New York to hear their take on this."

The screen cut to a series of interviews.

A middle-age woman with a baby in her arms, standing outside a housing project in Harlem. "I knew they were covering it up when they said that killer cop was dead." She spoke with an unimpressed tone. "Covering up for their own is just what those pigs do. Now he's doing it again . . . I bet they don't even want to catch the—"

BEEEEP, the censorship tone sounded over her swearing.

Christian Francis

An old man playing chess at a table in central park shook his head. "The cops? I wouldn't pick up the phone to call those fascists for anything. They'd probably just come over and kill me. Say I was a drug dealer, just 'cause of the color of my skin."

A female transient, sat alongside her ramshackle cardboard shelter, slurred drunkenly, "Cops have been killing people for years, and nobody cared then. Long as it was poor people they killed or street people. Who cared how many of them the cops knocked off? Right? But that it's a higher class of people dying, folks the cops think are better than us. So, *now* you hear about it. It *BEEEEP*-ing bull-*BEEEEP*."

A psychiatrist in his office, behind his desk, spoke with authority. "This is not a new phenomenon. The police in this city have a murky history if you look at the records. Going back to cops moonlighting as hitmen for the mob. Some just join the ranks of the NYPD as a way to access victims easier. Besides, speaking purely clinically, what it takes to be a cop and what it takes to be a murderer is, sadly, not that dissimilar."

A kid stood on the graffiti-strewn banks underneath the Manhattan side of the Brooklyn Bridge as a group of skateboards sped over the concrete behind him. He shrugged as he half looked into the camera. "We don't need no cops," he said in a strong Jersey accent. "We got to settle stuff ourselves, with our own weapons. That's how come a lot of people in this city got guns now. 'Cause we always knew cops would let us down in the end. And for the record, I don't think it's one cop that's doing this killing. It's a bunch of *BEEEEP*-ing cops."

Behind the counter of a gun store, a middle-aged woman with a strong Puerto Rican accent shook her head. "I'm more afraid of these police than I am of the muggers and the rapists. These police, they're loco with power. They want to scare us with these killings. They say, 'Look, it's okay. There is less crime on the streets now!'" she grimaced in disapproval. "Sure. Everybody stays in. They are afraid to go out! Now they see all the police, they run in the other direction. I came to this country to escape the bad cops. But they are here, too. And they like it like that. They like it that we fear them!" she sighed taking a look around her store at the many racks of guns. "But I gotta say, it is good for business. *Very* good. When a killer is on the streets, we sell many guns."

McKinney sat in his office as the television report played quietly in the background. On his desk, a half dozen newspapers lay face up. Their headlines staring at him as he scanned them, one by one. An annoyed grimace on his face as he did.

He was too engrossed to not hear Susan Riley walk in.

"Did you like my little appearance on TV?" she asked, unable to hide her smug grin.

McKinney glanced up and saw her standing defiantly in front of his desk. She wore a tough expression that McKinney greatly approved of, even if he could never say it to her. He noticed the bandage on her head was gone and that the wound on her forehead was visible. Stitched up and angry-looking. Her arm was also dangling out of the sling, though still in the plaster.

"You play up your injuries for the audience, huh?" he asked with a grin.

"Every little helps." She shrugged, not allowing his jibe to rattle her.

McKinney sighed. "Well, I'm not gonna lie to you. I loved you on that show. The mayor loved you. The city council? I think they may be your biggest fans." He picked up a newspaper and turned it around for her to see. "Check out the reviews."

"NYPD COVER-UP, Maniac Cop claims four more victims," it blared up at her.

"I guess I really started something." She smiled.

"You sure did."

"Maybe I should go home and wait for the ace to fall. Only a matter of time before they arrest me for breach of . . . whatever. Or try to silence me some other way. Arrest me for public endangerment."

"That genie is well and truly out of the bottle. But you gotta keep remembering. It's not like you made the genie." He stood from his desk, piling the newspapers

neatly. "But you won't be going home. Not with what's
out there. I'm putting you into protective custody."

Maniac Cop 2

neatly. "But you won't be going home. Not with what's out there. I'm putting you into protective custody."

"So, no more television?"

McKinney ignored the sarcastic question. "It's in order to keep you alive." He paused as his demeanor softened. "And I'm sorry about Mallory. I didn't really know her, but she seemed tough. And I respected that. And because of her, what happened to her, I have to protect you."

"You think Cordell has a reason to come after me?"

"No idea," He shrugged. "But if he doesn't come after you, I wouldn't put it past the commissioner to come and shoot you himself." He smiled at his own joke for a brief second. "This whole city is freaked the fuck out over that maniac cop. They all have this syndrome, where they'll shoot you even if you give them a bad feeling. Happened eighteen months ago, happening again now. But now, everyone seems more on edge."

"Where am I gonna go, then? A safe house?"

"Nothing as fancy, I'm afraid. I can't trust that this guy doesn't have an inside track on all our activity, so I got an extra room in my house. I don't have my address in the police system. So, anyone on the force won't be able to access that information."

"Where do your checks go?"

McKinney smiled. "PO Box."

Susan paused before changing the subject. "So, you believe me about all this?"

123

"I believe you. And I believe there is a cop out there killing. But there is no real evidence. Even so, if he *is* a cop, and he *is* Matthew Cordell, we just gotta make sure we're smart and not just playing into his hands. This guy faked his own death from a prison . . . I've been looking into it all. And I read Mallory and Jack Forrest's old reports and that of Detective Frank McCrae. All of them said they shot this asshole point blank. Swore he got up from even multiple head shots. Not to mention going under in the Hudson. Whatever he's doing, it's making him seem like he's dead already and coming back from the grave. I'm not saying that's the case, just that it is what it seems to be. So, I'll admit it, it's not safe at mine, but it's better than a custody place we have registered." He saw Susan looking troubled by his words. "You okay?"

"I don't know," she replied. "It's all this talk of Cordell being dead but still walking . . . Reminded me of an old rhyme I used to say when I was a kid in Brooklyn. A stupid, nonsense thing, but with all this bullshit, it keeps coming back. Haunting me . . ." She took a breath as if these words carried weight. "One bright day in the middle of the night, two dead boys got up to fight. Back-to-back, they faced each other. With their knives, they shot each other. A deaf policeman heard the noise and came and killed the two dead boys—"

"If you don't believe this lie is true"—McKinney smiled with a nod—"ask the blind man. He saw it too . . . Yeah, I get it. This whole thing is nonsense. If it doesn't make sense, then it could be that there is no sense to make. Or it's a damn good ruse. Think about it. All reports have said this guy has a big scarred head. That could be a mask, right? Like a protective one with some kind of armor plating. Hence the bullets not killing him. There's so much we don't know."

"So, what now?"

McKinney motioned to an old cracked leather sofa at one side of his office. "You can kick your legs up there for a bit. Stay here tonight, as I gotta work . . . But I'll order some food from the deli. You want anything from there? The Novia Scotia's damn good."

Susan never even considered food. But as she did, her belly ached. She had been in so much pain from the accident she did not even realize how hungry she was. Or how tired. She needed food and caffeine. She had to stay awake. She needed to. "Can I get a BLT and a coffee . . . lots of coffee?"

McKinney nodded with a smile and left the office.

The past forty-eight hours had been awful for her. Painful. Terrifying. Horrific. And she was in the grizzled cop's office, feeling the ache of her injuries, hoping for her meds to kick in a bit faster.

She had not felt that tired until she sat on the sofa, and she felt her heartbeat slow for maybe the first time since the accident. Then something happened that had not occurred since before her meeting with Matthew Cordell. She fell asleep. Passed out into unconsciousness by the sheer mental and physical exhaustion. She could not stop it from happening here if she tried.

Turkell was still sitting on the small chair in his apartment, opposite Matthew Cordell, who was sitting on the sofa, almost dwarfing it due to his size. His eight-point hat was removed and rested on a small coffee table next to his billy club. The light in the room high-lighted the extent of the injuries all over his head.

"They sure did a number on you, didn't they?" Turkell muttered with a chuckle. "I read about you back in the day. You were an honest cop, right? And they threw you in jail for, what, doing your job? Didn't they say excessive force or some shit? What did they expect? You fight fire with fire, not goddamn feathers." He leaned forward in his chair and took a closer look at Cordell's face, at the one bulging eye, the other sunken one. The huge dry deep gouges over his cheeks. The cavernous hole in place of his nose. Turkell studied his face more in admiration than curiosity. "You know what they say, right? Your scars make you. You look like total fear now. You've become fear. I would *love* to have that." He stared closer at the monster's eyes. "I've never seen anyone punished that much and still be able to breathe, still be able to walk around . . . Just like nothing happened."

Cordell didn't answer. He stared back. Behind his

eyes, though, was a nightmare being played out. A repeating kaleidoscope of his past.

He saw himself. The powerful man who was Matthew Cordell, enter the shower block at Sing Sing Penitentiary. He saw himself turn and the inmates, each carrying their own homemade weapons. Shivs, blades, and heavier blunt objects. He felt the same thing he had felt back then. A confusion, not a surprise, that, for the first time in his life, he could not beat away what was about to happen to him, not through want of trying, though. After a couple of retaliatory punches, the blades then came in. The sharpened toothbrush handles, the razor blades. Each came at him from every angle as they cut, stabbed and sliced his flesh mercilessly.

He had tried to fight. He had broken one man's arm over the edge of a shower cubicle. He had smashed another's face into the tile wall. Crushing his skull in one move. He had even shattered another's jaw with a frantic right-hand blow. But now, he was outnumbered and could only move so fast. The attack soon took its toll as wound after wound appeared over his body. And the more that came, the pain began to get debilitating. Finally, he could not stand, and he collapsed to his knees in the shower. The water had fallen down on him from the running head above, washing the blood away as the men continued their tirade upon his body.

He had felt the moment his nose was hacked off with one of the razors. A single slice of the homemade weapon was all it took for the whole of his thing to be cut away and fall down into where his arms lolled. He remembered the feeling of that small chunk of flesh and gristle landing in his open palm. He even had the foresight to try and save his nose during this barrage of violence, balling his fist around it, in the hope it could maybe be reattached if he survived. He remembered the man's face who did it. Leering at him with joyful sadism.

Then the heavy objects came. The metal mallet stolen from the workshop that slammed into his eye socket, cracking it on impact. The metal pipe taken from one of the showers, smacking into his spine.

As Cordell sat in Turkell's apartment, he remembered being murdered in such vivid detail. There was no way he could not. It was the only image that was in his mind, and that memory remained as vivid to him as when it happened. The haunting of it never left him, nor did the pain of when it happened. All Cordell could feel was that moment and the rage that followed.

Susan slept on the sofa in McKinney's office. In her dreams, she became plagued with her own version of what Cordell had gone through, having heard about it from Teresa. She had never seen the showers in Sing Sing, she had never seen Cordell's face as it was before his attack, but here, she stood in witness at the event. All through her own lens.

The shower room in her nightmare was surreal. With a ceiling so high that it disappeared into a deep darkness, and from within, a shower of water poured down from an unseen height. As if each brick made cubicle reached up to the sky and the shower had been its own confined rainstorm.

The floor here was also slicked with a few inches of blood. A thick pool that Matthew Cordell stood within. Naked but with his face unseen. He was not alone. He was fighting against an onslaught of horned demons. Each carried with them large ceremonial daggers in their clawed grips.

Before the dreamscape version of Susan could discern what was happening, she ran between the demons and Cordell as if trying to protect him. The same man who murdered countless people.

She threw a punch toward one of the attackers, smashing it in the side of the head. The dagger it held fell to the bloody pool beneath her. Frantically, she bent down and scooped the weapon in her hand, then turned it back on the demon, thrusting it forward with a tremendous cry.

As the blade split into its flesh, she saw that this was not a demon she attacked but, instead, was Detective Lieutenant Sean McKinney. Dressed in a ceremonial black robe, with the look of a petrified child as he gasped for breath. He then collapsed forward, into her arms.

"Why," he spluttered as blood gushed out between his lips, grappling at the dagger deep in his belly.

"No," Susan suddenly cried out at what she had just done. "Please, no!"

Behind them, Cordell continued fighting off his own demons, creating their own terrible roars of anger.

But through her cries, through these demons' roars, through McKinney's gargled spluttering, there was something else . . . The sound of children. Young children speaking in unison. In rhyme.

"The deaf policeman heard the noise, Came and shot the two dead boys . . ."

Susan's eyes snapped open as she gasped for breath, dragged from her nightmare by her own fear.

"Your lunch came," McKinney said, sitting at his desk and chewing on a sandwich. He motioned to the paper bag on a table by her head.

Grasping herself back into reality, she stared at the bag, then back to McKinney. "Why didn't you wake me?"

"You looked peaceful." He shrugged with a laugh. "Besides, that's the longest I've seen you quiet for."

"Hey," Detective Lovejoy said, leaning into the office, "you wanted to know when that stripper was here . . . . Well, she's down in the cafeteria waiting for you. Just got out of the hospital."

Nodding his thanks, McKinney looked at Susan.

"You should come down too. I think you'll wanna hear this."

In the cafeteria, Cheryl Dandridge sat nervously. A world away from her appearance as Miss Lenore, she was dressed in a jumper and sweat pants, without make up and with deep bruises around her throat. As she cradled a cup of coffee, each sip she had swallowed had been painful, but she wanted to beat this. She wouldn't be ruled by what happened. The detective had asked if she would be willing to help, and she was. She would do all she could to stop any of this happening again. She survived what happened, and she believed it must have been for a reason.

Lovejoy and McKinney walked in, closely followed by Susan.

"Ms. Dandridge," Lovejoy said with a smile. "You know Detective Lieutenant McKinney, and this is Officer Susan Riley."

"I'm not an officer," Susan corrected.

"But you *are* a cop," McKinney said. "Whether you have an actual rank or not."

Cheryl smiled thinly, greeting them all.

Lovejoy turned to Susan. "Ms. Dandridge here was attacked yesterday evening by someone we believe murdered all the exotic dancers across the city."

"I only danced once," Cheryl said, her voice broken

and wheezing through her injuries. "It's not what I do. Not who I am."

Susan was confused. "How am I supposed to help in this?" she asked Lovejoy.

"Tonight, we're gonna hit some of the similar clubs in lower Manhattan," Lovejoy explained. ". . . And Ms. Dandridge here has agreed to come along to identify her assailant. We believe he goes to these clubs often. So, if he chooses any of the ones we're staking out, we can catch him before he does it again."

"We'll be going in and out of these places, pretending to be couples," McKinney added. "Lovejoy and Ms. Dandridge here. And me and . . . Well, we need a policewoman."

"Me?" Susan asked aghast. "Why me? I'm injured, not to mention there are loads of other officers who've way more experience in this than I do. I'm just a psychologist."

McKinney smiled. Savoring the reveal. "Ms. Dandridge's attacker here, well . . . he was rescued that night. Ms. Dandridge? Care to describe the man?"

Cheryl, though not knowing what was happening, did as she was asked. "He was a huge cop. He looked like a monster . . . and he stank. Well, they both stank."

"Killed two cops as well." McKinney nodded. "We put out a story that Ms. Dandridge here died en route to Bellevue so her attacker wouldn't try and find her and finish the job."

Susan stared down at Cheryl as she noticed her

bruises. "If you don't mind me asking, did the cop do that to your throat?"

Cheryl nodded, slightly uncomfortable. "Both had a go."

Susan continued. "What did they feel like—his hands, I mean? If you don't mind me asking."

"I only remember they were really cold and so big." Cheryl took another painful sip of her coffee.

"You wanna come along now? In case Cordell shows?" McKinney asked. "Remember, I'll be there, so you'll be protected. I'll also issue you a weapon."

Susan sighed. "Bullets do nothing except get his attention, and you *don't* want that."

Turkell had fallen asleep on the stained mattress in his apartment as a loud creak from the front door woke him. Blearily, he looked across the murky room and saw Cordell opening the front door.

"Wait," Turkell called out, scrambling to his feet. "Don't you go leaving me!" He sounded increasingly desperate. "It's not safe out there!"

Cordell, though, did not listen. He just strode out and didn't look back.

"Going someplace I can't go, huh?" Turkell said as he got to the door.

Cordell was walking across the dark alleyway beside the apartment. "You'll come back, alright?"

Turkell shouted after the Maniac Cop, but he disappeared around a corner.

Feeling suddenly alone and restless, Turkell glanced into his apartment, then back out into the empty alley. "Well, I guess I better find something to do as well." He walked back in and grabbed his Polaroid camera from the sideboard, but before he left, he caught sight of his face in a mirror. Staring for a moment, he put his hand over his nose as he pictured himself without it. As he imagined his face like Cordell's.

At this late hour across Times Square and nearby streets, the nightlife pulsed with a seedy energy. Sex arcades, strip clubs, and porn theaters lined the sidewalks, their blinking marquees advertising more than they could ever possibly give as their glow reflected off the hoods of passing vehicles.

"No admission, no cover," a man in a cheap suit shouted from outside a club, breaking through the hum of the nightlife. "Two-drink minimum. See New York's most beautiful women . . . in the flesh! You want pussy, we got pussy. You want ass, we got ass. You want something else? Well, if you got the money, we got what you need!"

As the man spoke, his eyes scanned the crowds for hesitant or lonely souls with full wallets looking for a cheap thrill. He offered the wares insides to businessmen, drifters, as well as wide-eyed newcomers. All were welcome.

The air billowing around each club was thick with cigarette smoke, exhaust fumes, and the lingering scent of semen.

Susan, McKinney, Cheryl, and Lovejoy had spent the last couple of hours moving from club to club, studying the patrons within. Each of the people they saw had faces with traces of loneliness and desperation upon them. And all looked even more lonely and frustrated when they left, for none of them got what they wanted. None were offered actual sex. Just the tease of it. The lure of it. For anything more, they would need to walk beyond the nicer clubs and into the more desperate parts of the city, where bodies were for rent at much lower prices than it was to view them around these streets.

Through all the seedy stained clubs, Cheryl had not seen her assailant or even one that looked remotely similar. After walking back to the unmarked sedan, McKinney got behind the wheel as the others got in the passenger seats. They each felt somewhat deflated at the night's failures. But the night was not yet over. They had another red-light district in lower Manhattan to visit. A much cheaper and more desperate set of strip clubs.

As the sedan rolled away, its taillights faded down the long stretch of street, none of its passengers inside had heard the faint whistling that drifted on the wind from a side street, moving in the opposite direction.

Through the shadows, past rows of overflowing trash, Matthew Cordell slowly walked. His broken mouth whistled the same six discordant notes, over and over. He didn't know why or how—he just was. Somewhere, buried beneath the endless nightmare reel of his own murder being replayed in his mind, a distant memory had surfaced. An image of himself, once whole, walking these same streets on beat. Back then, though, the tune had been in key. And as he walked, he may not have known why he whistled that same tune, but he did so anyway.

Chapter 7

Just down from Avenue B and East 2nd Street, away from the classier, more known adult establishments like The Gas Station, The Velvet Hole was a low-rent dive where the dancers doubled as prostitutes when the offers arose. It was a place that reeked of sweat and lube, where shoes stuck to the linoleum with each footstep.

In this club, unlike the others, each table had its own podium, where dancers performed just for the individuals sitting there. It was up-close, raw, and not for the faint of heart.

Cheryl led the way through the half-crowded room as McKinney dawdled by the entrance, paying the cover charge for all four of them.

"Looking for a bit of spice for your date, eh?" the sleazy doorman asked. "We can get you what ya want.

Want some marching powder to make it all a buzz? Just ask."

It took every ounce of McKinney's willpower to not lean across and drag the man to the police station for booking. But, tonight, he had to remember it wasn't about a low-level drug offense or anything as petty as solicitation. It was about murder. So, he had to let it all go and just smile politely.

"Maybe later," McKinney replied before walking into the club after the other three, toward a corner table where the rest all sat.

As they each surveyed the venue, a bored-looking server walked up with four sloppily filled complimentary glasses of beer.

Around her, the customers enjoying their shows were quite vocal. They cheered and whooped at the dancers, offering them encouragement to take off more —or to jiggle more. As they thrust dollar bills into the girls' garters, cleavage, or anywhere else they could reach.

The lights in the club blinked in pinks and purples as cigarette smoke filled the air. The music they all danced to was almost at deafening levels.

"Looks like hard work," Lovejoy said loudly as he watched one dancer lower her bare breasts onto a patron's ecstatic, awaiting face.

Cheryl may not have been a seasoned pro, but she knew enough dancers. She had heard all the stories. Not only had she worked as a server, but she also lived in the same building as many of the workers. It's why she had decided to dance in the first place. "A girl can clear a thousand bucks a week with tips. And that's without offering any extras," she said to Lovejoy. "How much do *you* clear a week, huh?"

"She's got you there," McKinney laughed, over-hearing. "Maybe you should take up dancing lessons?"

Susan tugged on Cheryl's arm to get her attention. "See anyone familiar?"

"No," Cheryl replied. "A few creeps I've seen at other clubs but not him."

They sat there for a few minutes in silence, staring. This was the fifth club they had walked into, and at each one they had walked in, they sat and surveyed the area. Never staying in them for long. If Cheryl could not see the man, they moved to the next. They had many bars to cover and little time.

"Shall we?" Susan said.

"Yeah, good idea," Lovejoy added as he stared at the dirty glass his beer had been served in. "Let's vamoose before we catch something."

Before he could stand, Lovejoy gawked as a dancer approached and climbed up on the podium in front of their table. She then began gyrating her groin toward him.

"Wanna fuck me?" the stripper said loudly, licking her lips at him. "Maybe if you're a good, good boy!"

McKinney, Lovejoy, and Susan all stared up in half shock and half horror. Not knowing how to handle this.

Christian Francis

That night, they were undercover, but this was too close and real.

Cheryl chuckled, finding their reactions very entertaining. So much so that she did not notice a new entrant to the club. A bedraggled, hairy man with rotten teeth. It was Stephen Turkell. He was there for a moment, then lost among the crowd.

Lovejoy's shock slowly turned to an embarrassed grin as her thrusting got closer and closer to him.

At the bar, Turkell struggled to get the bartender's attention, with the music being so loud and the other patrons being significantly more forceful and confident with their orders.

"Cutty Sark on the rocks," he shouted loudly across the bar, to no avail. "Hey!" he shouted again, louder as he waved his hand. "Cutty . . . Rocks!"

But everyone there was screaming for their orders, so his voice got lost. The bartender was either speaking to the loudest or being distracted by the dancer's near hardcore displays.

Turkell continued to wait for the man to look his way. Getting more annoyed the more he stood there.

"Better give her a tip," Cheryl said to Lovejoy as he was staring, wide-eyed and mesmerized, at the dancer nearly on top of him.

"C'mon, let's just go," McKinney grumbled while standing, having had enough of these places. "Leave the drinks."

It wasn't that he was a prude; he just was so focused on his job, nothing else mattered.

A long mirror stretched across the back of the bar, affording Turkell a view of the whole floor while not having to turn around. He glanced at his own reflection, looking annoyed as he was still being ignored by the bartender.

As he turned to try and get a drink one more time, Turkell's eyes glimpsed something. *Someone.*

Only visible for a second.

No, it can't be. Can it?

But where he had seen them, a man stood in a long black trench coat, wearing a fedora, blocking his line of sight.

Shaking off this confusion, Turkell turned back to the bartender and screamed again as loud as he could. "Cutty. Fucking. Sark. On the. Fucking. Rocks. *Please.*"

Hearing this, the bartender nodded blankly and grabbed a glass to fill his order.

Turkell's thoughts sank back to what he just thought he saw. *That couldn't have been her*, he mused. *She died.* He had seen what Cordell did to that woman, and there was no way she could have survived that.

Was there?

"Your scotch," the Bartender said as he placed a glass on the bar in front of him. "Hello? Fella? Your drink!"

But Turkell was distracted. He faced the other way, consumed by his thoughts. He then walked away from the bar, leaving his drink and the bartender through a throng of men crowding near him. He had to see. He had to know.

"Hey, asshole," one man seethed as Turkell barged by, knocking on his drink. But Turkell did not stop or engage, he just had to push through to see what he thought he saw.

Just as the man in the coat and fedora moved, Turkell's eyes widened in anticipation, but the dancer on the table stepped off and stood in his way.

A nervous sweat quickly broke out over his body. As his breathing quickened, he pushed past more patrons.

"Cool it, ya bum," one shouted.

Cordell wouldn't have this problem, Turkell thought with a pang of envy. *People were afraid of him on sight.*

Cheryl, Lovejoy, and Susan stood to walk away with McKinney, but as they did, Cheryl glanced across the club and immediately froze. With the other three moving to the exit, she was left by the table.

She saw *him*, and more horrifyingly, he saw her.

She had thought that she was strong enough for this. She thought that she could fight back and help catch this murderer. But here, staring at him. Seeing him staring back at her with his cruel eyes, she felt like she was back there in her apartment. With him on top of her once again. Breathing on her, rubbing against her. Salivating on her.

There was no doubt in Turkell's mind. It *was* her.

"Hey, buddy!" the bartender shouted from behind. "You left your drink!"

Susan, realizing Cheryl was not behind her, turned to see what was happening. She quickly noticed Cheryl's fear paralyzing her to the spot as she stared into the crowd.

"McKinney!" she called back, knowing exactly what was happening.

As he heard and looked past Susan to Cheryl, he didn't need any instruction.

But they were on the opposite side of the club. The music pounded too loudly to shout over.

McKinney motioned to Lovejoy to circle to the bar alongside him. To approach whatever she stared at from behind.

. . .

Turkell was about to advance on Cheryl, when a big hand reached out and grabbed him tightly by the arm.

"Pick up your drink from the bar and pay the six bucks!" the bartender ordered, having walked out from behind his station after him. *"Now!"*

At that moment, Turkell noticed McKinney and Lovejoy making their way over, looking alert and focused. He knew that kind of look a mile off. They had a cop's look.

This was a trap.

But the bartender had an immense grip on Turkell's arm and was not intending to let go.

In a sudden panic, Turkell elbowed the man in the groin, sending him doubled over downward. Scurrying ahead a few steps, Turkell lunged toward a dancer on a nearby podium. Obliviously gyrating, she had no idea of what was happening as Turkell shoved her hard from behind, sending her screaming down, crashing onto the approaching Lovejoy and blocking McKinney's route.

The closely packed crowd of men jostled about in confusion, trying to figure out what was going on amid the volume of the music and blaring of the lights.

Turkell did not wait. He pushed, kicked, and punched his way through the mob as fast as he could.

The bartender, back on his feet, raced toward him, but Turkell was too quick. He sensed the bartender's approach, grabbed a beer bottle from a nearby table, and swung it with no compunction across the bartender's face. The glass smashed on impact, knocking the man down and out.

Time then slowed down for Turkell as he looked around, searching for any escape route. But there were people everywhere, blocking his view. He had no time. He had to think of something. He had to . . .

Cordell.

His face scared everyone away.

With a quick smile and not even pausing for thought, Turkell gripped onto the remnants of the bottle and raised it to his face.

Screams and panic ensued as the surrounding crowd witnessed in terror what Turkell had begun to do to himself. The dense huddle of men and dancers began to scream and rush to the exit as they saw him lift the glass up to his nose and begin to cut into his own face, all the while laughing maniacally.

Quickly, the crowd around him thinned as it pushed back.

McKinney, Lovejoy, and Cheryl could not see what was going on through the furor, but Susan did. She had managed to catch a glimpse of Turkell, rushing over the bar and heading for the fire escape on the far side of the club. The side of the club she was on. She then saw something on his face. A flash of red. Dismissing the thought, she then hurried up and over a group of tables and ran through a line of panicked dancers who raced for the exit. She had managed to reach the far end of the club before Turkell has finished scrambling over. And he had not seen her as he approached. He had not even clocked her as one of the cops.

Through the blood pouring down his face and the ice-cold pain searing through his body, Turkell sensed no threat in Susan as he passed her.

But with her hand and wrist in a heavy plaster cast, she had a weapon molded to her arm. Before she could focus on the details of his face, she swung her arm like a club, slamming it across the back of his head.

As Turkell crumbled to the stained carpeted floor, she let out a painful scream as the plaster on her arm cracked on impact.

Cheryl was still staring as most of the crowd left, and McKinney and Lovejoy walked over to where Turkell lay in a daze. Her fear soon turned to curiosity as she noticed that each of them had looked down at Turkell with a look of utter revulsion as Lovejoy turned and vomited at what he just saw.

There, lying on the filthy, sticky floor of this dive strip joint, Stephen Turkell grinned inanely, his lips sliced back over bloodied teeth. His face was a mass of self-inflicted violence, deep gouges carved into his skin by the jagged edge of the broken beer bottle. The wounds oozed dark, thick blood that pooled on the carpet beneath his trembling body. His nose, barely clinging to his face by the thinnest sinewy strands, exposed the dark nasal passageway below. One of his eyes had also been punctured. The deflated ball leaked a thick, gelatinous fluid outward onto his sliced-up cheek.

But he was not in pain, not how most would feel it. He was beyond that. His breath came in gasps, blood gurgling in his throat as he laughed.

The rest of the patrons had fled, the dancers had rushed to hide in their small dressing rooms, yet the lights still spun and the music still blared, the emcee having run away. Even the security guards were outside, waiting for whatever was happening inside to finish. The trouble being more than their pay was worth.

McKinney, Susan, and Lovejoy remained there, Cheryl beside them. They stared down at Stephen who was lost in some unspeakable rapture. He lay there, grinning . . . . "I'm like you now," he gurgled. "We are the same."

"Bring the car round," McKinney said to Lovejoy, who was still feeling the turbulence within his guts.

"Not callin' an ambulance?" Susan asked.

"Doesn't look like he's severed an artery," McKinney replied dismissively. "He can see someone in booking to patch him up."

As he was picked off the floor, handcuffed, and made to stagger out on his own weakened and trembling legs, Turkell was a docile shell of what he felt inside. Inside, he was furious and ecstatic all at once. He was a storm of joy and anger that made him feel invincible. As he saw the looks of the people outside the club who screamed at his appearance, he could not help being turned on nor could he hide the indication bulging in his trousers.

With the blood seeping off him and his face a wreck of carved up violence, he felt like he had won. He may have been caught, but he felt *more* than he ever had done in the past. These people were not just afraid of him, but they were sickened, and even distraught at having to look at him.

Quickly, he was ushered into the backseat of the unmarked sedan, with McKinney in the middle and Susan pressed against the far door. Up front, Lovejoy slid behind the wheel while Cheryl settled into the passenger seat.

"You understand what I just said?" McKinney said as he concluded Turkell's Miranda rights.

Turkell smiled as he spat out a large globule of congealed blood from his mouth onto the floor. "I wanna see my lawyer," he said gleefully.

Lovejoy avoided looking at Turkell again, at that face that caused him to lose his dinner on the strip club floor. He just fought against his ill feeling and drove, moving the rearview to an angle which didn't show him the backseat.

Cheryl was the same. She could not look at the man who attacked her, as it was all too much. He had become even more of a monster, and the memories in her head had changed. On top of her, drooling, was the version of Turkell that sat in the back seat. It did not help that everyone could smell him. His stench of stale urine, sweat, and filth was almost blinding, but it was mixed by a warm coppery smell of blood. Lovejoy, Cheryl, and Susan each had their windows down, hoping for the fresh city air to wash this filthy odor away.

"What happened to your friend?" McKinney questioned. "The big cop. Where'd he go?"

This was the reason he didn't want an ambulance to pick up Turkell. He didn't want to miss a moment questioning him.

Turkell smiled and let out a gurgled chuckle. "My friend? He's my friend all right. He won't forget about me. You'll see."

Susan summoned all of her strength and peered around McKinney to look at the newly disfigured murderer. "Did you do that to look like Cordell?"

"How do you know his—" Turkell's smile faltered for a second before returning just as quick. "Oh, right, you! You're the one who was on *Criminals At Large*. Didn't recognize you without the bandage. Thought your injury would be bigger, though," he added, nodding to her stitched head wound. "We look kind of the same now." He laughed, but as he did, the adrenaline started to wear off, and the pain in his face began to come to the forefront. He tried his best to keep on track. "You . . . you think you can stop . . . him? Some

149

lousy show can't get in his way. A bunch of two-bit cops in a beat-up heap of junk like this? You all got a big surprise coming."

In the basement level of 1 Police Plaza was the largest holding facility in New York. For most, it was a quick stop while being arraigned before being turfed out to a larger jail, like Riker's Island. In one of the cells in a room of about a dozen, Turkell sat still, handcuffed, his face fully bandaged. Only one eye, his ears, mouth, and some tufts of hair could be seen poking out between the wrappings. He was heavily medicated and almost delirious with glee.

"Did you save me my nose like I asked?" he asked McKinney, who was standing outside the cell, looking in. "I wanna make it a necklace or something."

"Oh, right. Yeah. I'll get *right* on that," McKinney said as he shook his head. "You'll be happy to know that you should be fine. Doc said nothing you've done is life threatening unless you get an infection. So, you'll be transferred to a secure hospital facility as soon as we get you a bed. Got it?"

Turkell didn't reply, just grinned under the glow of the painkillers, staring at his captor.

McKinney then held up a wallet, Turkell's wallet, and showed it the prisoner. "Got your driver's license in here. That your current address?"

Turkell still grinned silently back.

. . .

Exiting the cells and going back into the main foyer, McKinney noticed Susan waiting for him by the door.

"Haven't you seen enough action tonight?" he said with a smile. "You all good?"

"Just got this replastered," she said as she held up her fresh arm. "You need me for anything else?"

"Nah, I got a whole squad going to that piece of shit's house," he replied. "You should go sleep. You got the keys to my place and my address. Just let yourself in. Spare room is first on the right as you go in. I can get a squad car to escort you there to be safe."

"I don't think I can sleep now," she said. "Maybe I'll go down to the range and practice a few. Improve my aim."

"Under the circumstances, I think that's wise. Can't go clobbering all the bad guys with your broken wrist!"

Two hours later, Susan was in the small firing range in the upper level of 1 Police Plaza. With the gun that McKinney requisitioned for her firmly in her grip, ear defenders and shooting glasses on, she aimed her barrel at the paper target. Adjusting her grip due to her plastered wrist.

Around her, a handful of other officers, uniformed

and plain clothed, took their time firing at targets at the far end of the room.

With only her right hand able to grip the gun tightly, she took aim at the target and fired a succession of three shots. Each was poorly spaced and had missed their intended targets. But all had hit the paper, though.

From behind her, Jim Dixon the range officer walked over. Having been signed off from patrol for emotional distress and reassigned to the range, Jim knew Susan well. She was his therapist during his transition from the beat to here, and he was very thankful to her for how she helped him. She was the one who fought for his transfer, and as a fifty-year-old cop, getting any relocation was not an easy ask. They would rather have gotten rid of him, but she had fought his corner and won. And he loved his new job here. It was calm, slow, and just a bit noisy.

"Straighten that elbow," he said.

Glancing around, Susan smiled as she saw Jim approach. "Guess I'm not as good as I used to be?"

"Wait, you used to be good at this?" he laughed. "When was that?"

"Well, *good* is a stretch, maybe *not as terrible* is more accurate!"

Jim stood beside her, looking at her target at the other end. "I guess you're better at shooting your mouth off on television," he quipped.

"I'm damn proud of that," she replied as she raised

her weapon and fired another three shots just as widely spaced and just as off target.

"Keep trying, Susan. You'll get the knack soon enough." He shrugged with a smile. "Maybe in a year or two. But for now, I think it's best you tell everyone you're left-handed and are shooting with your weaker arm."

The door to Turkell's apartment cracked open as an NYPD officer used a crowbar to break its lock. As the door swung inward, McKinney quickly stepped inside, his eyes sweeping the dimly lit and messy space as he searched for a light switch. Behind him, five other officers followed, all with their guns out, ready for any potential surprises. Within moments, the light had been switched on and the room was bathed in a dirty yellow glow, barely bright enough to see any real details.

As soon as they had entered the empty apartment, the acrid smell that lingered inside hit them. The same foul mix of waste and sweat that clung to Turkell was in force here.

"Make sure you all keep your gloves on," McKinney called out to his men. He gripped his gun in one hand and flashlight in the other as he looked around. "Aside from any evidence, no telling what you might catch from this shit tip."

Almost immediately, McKinney's noticed the pin

board of polaroids. The photos of Turkell's victims, taken in distress.

His reaction to this was a wide smile. "Gotcha," he muttered before turning to his squad. "We got ourselves a serial killer boys. So, by the book. Find, bag, log. Got it?"

Alone in his cell, Turkell sat on his bed with the thick bandages still wrapped around his head. Faint traces of blood seeped through the gauze in several places. He was twitchy as he tapped his foot onto the concrete floor. He was never a man in his right mind, but here, with the added trauma he put onto himself, his mind was slipping even further into the abyss.

"Don't leave me here," he mumbled, as if Cordell could somehow hear him. "You're gonna come for me, I know it! I'm waiting for you. I'm waiting for you, my friend."

"Shut the fuck up," said a gravelly voice from the next cell along, where a young, full-body tattooed man called Blum was trying to sleep. "At least I'll get some peace and quiet in Ossining."

Turkell stopped his mumbling and turned to the man. "Ossining? You going to Sing Sing?"

"Stalled the bastards from sending me down for five years," Blum grunted back. "Now they finally fucked me. And last thing I need is you babbling away to yourself when I'm trying to sleep!"

Turkell chuckled. "You should be nice to me. When he comes to break me out, I could take you along for the ride."

Blum turned over in his bed away from Turkell. "I won't hold my breath."

Turkell shook his head and turned his attention back to the front of the cell. "He'll come," he whispered. "You'll see. You'll all see!"

The door at the end of the room opened with a loud creak. Turkell did not look up and did not see Susan Riley approach until she stood in front of his cell.

"Stephen Turkell," she asked. "Can we talk?"

Without looking, he answered quietly. "What time is it?"

"Just after 9 p.m."

"Night owl, huh?" he asked. He then peered up to see her standing looking at him, with a look of discomfort on her face. He also noticed the bright new cast on her arm. "Want me to sign that?" he said as he let out a light chuckle.

Susan wasn't playing. "I want you to tell me about Cordell," she said emotionlessly. "You seem to know a lot about him. Even your cuts are in the same place as his. Are you trying to be him?"

This brought a smile to Turkell's face. Wide and displaying his stumps of rotten teeth. "You noticed? I hope he does, too . . . But if you want to know about him, just stick around here tonight. You'll sure as hell learn something."

The firing range, like the rest of the station, never closed. With all the twenty-four-seven shift patterns of the officers, someone was always in there practicing their aim. And at 9:11 p.m., three young trainee officers were firing at their individual targets, working overtime to make sure they excelled in their weapon proficiency.

One shot after another, they fired at the end for the range, into the paper targets. Around these sheets, illuminated from spot lights on the ceiling, was a deep shadow. Framing the bright targets for a better sight to aim at.

Jim Dixon was nearing the end of his long shift. He had been on duty for almost ten hours, he only had thirty-nine minutes left until the next range officer was due to clock on. It couldn't come fast enough for him.

He was staring into space, daydreaming of his bed, when one of the young officers suddenly stopped firing. He turned to Jim with a look of concern.

"Uh, sir?" the officer said. "I think there's someone down there."

Pushing himself off his chair, Jim stepped forward. "Cease fire! Cease fire! Cease fire!" he shouted to the other officers, over the sounds of their shots.

"I saw someone," the officer repeated as Jim stood beside him, looking down the range.

"Where?" Jim asked.

"They walked across the back when I stopped firing."

Just what he needed at the end of a long shift. He had seen this kind of thing before, rookies playing tricks on each other. Hiding at the back, having coming through the back door, hiding out of view and out of the bullet fire, only to jump out and scare the trainees. Luckily, since he had worked here, no one had died or got seriously injured from this.

"Come on, who's out there?" Jim shouted into the shadows at the end of the room. The other officers had stopped shooting and were staring into the darkness beyond the targets, squinting to see what may be there.

"You wanna get yourself killed, huh?" Jim continued. "Come out, and I won't report you."

Silence.

Then . . .

Bang!

A shot rang out but not from the shooting gallery but from the target area. A loud shot from out of the shadows. The fired bullet zipped out of the darkness and through the eye of the young officer standing next to Jim, cracking through his shooting glasses and blowing a cavernous hole in the back of his skull, spilling his brains in seared chunks all over the wall behind him.

Jim and the other officers barely had time to react as, from out of the darkness, a large figure emerged.

Matthew Cordell. The Maniac Cop. A still smoking revolver in his gloved hand. Walking slowly, purposefully, toward them.

"Return fire! Now!" Jim shouted with urgency to the trainees as he grabbed the weapon from the fallen officer's hand and turned it toward this intruder.

The wave of bullets that flew toward Cordell were perfectly aimed. The two officers and Jim fired with high accuracy at the approaching man. Bullet after bullet pierced through Cordell's chest, head, legs. Every point on the body that could disable or kill a man was quickly hit. But not one of these shots seemed to slow the target down. He just kept coming. This great monolith of a monster just kept coming. His slow and steady pace not faltering even for one second.

Cordell didn't fire another shot until he was within three feet of the gallery, and when he did, the bullet blasted out and tore though Jim's throat, sending him hurtling backward, his body crumpling to the carpet as blood jettisoned out of his wound, pooling in his lungs and violently drowning him. A shot that was inevitable in its conclusion but would take a couple of minutes to complete. A couple of minutes where Jim gasped to breathe, unable to do anything except lie there, terrified at his own ending life.

"I hit that bastard in the goddamn face!" one of the

officers shouted, backing away as Cordell stepped over the gallery partition.

"Run!" the other shouted.

With two quick successive shots, Cordell aimed his gun and fired. One bullet for each of the escaping officers' head. Killing them both instantly.

As Cordell stepped next to Jim, he stared down at his gasping body. With neither sadism nor pity, Cordell's next movement was purely completion of his work as his boot came down upon Jim's head. Demolishing it into the carpet with one skull-crushing stomp.

Before any alarms could be raised, two officers were walking up to the firing range, ready to get some practice in. From where they were, they could not hear the massacre in the soundproof room.

As they turned the corner, up the final flight to the range, the door ahead of them flew open, hitting the exposed concrete brick behind it with a loud thud.

These officers only had time to grab the hilts of their weapons before Cordell appeared and fired his gun toward them.

Bang! Bang! One shot after the other in another quick succession, this time between the eyes of each officer. Executing them with precision.

They tumbled back down the stairs, dead.

. . .

In the main offices of the building, Detective Lovejoy was still working at his desk. Having booked in Stephen Turkell, he had a mountain of paperwork to fill in. He was at least glad he didn't have to babysit Cheryl Dandridge any more. She had been given a police escort back to her apartment hours ago as her attacker was safely caught and behind bars. But with Cordell still at large, the escorting officers would need to stand watch outside her door for a few days, ensuring she was in no further danger.

With those officers busy and McKinney still searching the killer's home with the rest of the team, it was all down to Lovejoy to get a start on the countless forms and statements of what had happened.

Normally, he would love this assignment, far away from the death. Away from the blood. Away from the violence. Sitting in the safety of the office. But all he could see as he wrote his statement of what went down at The Velvet Glove was Turkell's decimated face. The face with long open wounds all over it. His punctured eye. His carved off nose that dangled as if it were on a fleshy string. Even the memory of it made his stomach turn.

He did not hear the shots from the stairwell. The walls were too thick here to hear anything from outside of them. And like Lovejoy, no one working late in these offices had any idea of what just transpired upstairs, not until the door to the staircase opened.

In the doorway, Matthew Cordell stood under the

bright, unforgiving fluorescent strip light, gun in hand as he glanced around the open-plan offices. At first, people just saw the uniform he wore and thought nothing else. But it only took a glance for an extra second to notice the huge size of the man, the mauled features on his face, the mold and blood that covered his clothes. He may not have worn a badge anymore, not after losing it at the Pier 18 months ago, but he was still obviously a cop. A cop whose gun lifted and aimed toward them.

Chapter 8

Chaos reigned as Matthew Cordell fired shots at every person in the main offices of 1 Police Plaza. Policemen, suspects, cleaners, visitors . . . It didn't matter. As he fired shot after shot, he did not choose who his victims were. He just saw a target and fired. Each bullet accurate as a kill shot for each trigger finger. And when his gun was emptied, he reloaded from bullets in his jacket pocket.

Officers tried to fire back and defend themselves, but Cordell was unrelenting. When he focused on his next target, he stormed toward them, and they did not stand a chance. One female officer only managed to fire a single shot before he was upon her. He slammed his fists on either side of her face, cracking her head inward with the brute force. He then grabbed the weapon from her deathly convulsing hand and fired its remaining bullets at more people as they ran for cover.

Among them was Detective Lovejoy, who threw himself under a nearby desk.

One tough sergeant, known for his strength and uncompromising nature, was also there and would not let someone like Cordell just come into his station and kill. No. He would grab his gun and—

Too late.

The Maniac Cop was in front of him, ramming his fist into the tough cop's breastplate, crushing it inward. In one movement, Cordell's hand was inside the tough man's torso, grabbing all the organs he could grasp and ripping them out. As he did, the man's heart and lungs were ripped out and his body then hurled across the room. It didn't matter who you were or what you were like—Matthew Cordell was unstoppable and brutal.

The glass partitions between the offices could not slow him down, either. He barreled straight through them like a juggernaut, shards billowing down like rain around him as he cut short another person's life.

So many bullets were fired at him, and all these shots were wasted. For those brave enough to stay and fight, Cordell would soon be coming for them. If they stayed, they would not escape.

Matthew Cordell did not think about anything while he was exerting all of this violence on the station. He barely knew what he was doing. He was just functioning on pure rage. In his mind, all he knew was the torment from his own execution in the Sing Sing shower room.

A handful of people, though, managed to escape his wraith, getting to the exit before Cordell could make his way over to stop them. Lovejoy was among them.

As he ran, with tears streaming down his face in fear, Lovejoy could not think of anything except wanting to run and never stop.

"Are you *sure* it's only 9 p.m.?" Turkell asked Susan as a large smile decorated his face. "'Cause it sounds like out there it's visiting hours."

Unlike the soundproofed shooting range, the gunshots and crashes from the offices upstairs had been clearly heard in the cells below, alerting Susan not to mention the incarcerated inmates down with her.

It was only Turkell who did not have a look of shock, confusion or surprise to the cacophony.

"Hey, nice lady?" he called out. Stealing Susan's attention toward him. "My friend's back. You know that? So, you can ask him your questions yourself."

The screams of men and women gradually got closer from upstairs as the gunshots carried down the stairs, getting nearer and nearer to the cells. Something was headed this way.

Susan's fear flooded her as she stared at the ecstatic Turkell. "How is this possible?" she whimpered.

"Oh, that's easy," he replied. "Because he and I

need each other. He knows what I want—I know what he wants."

Susan ran to the doors and threw them open, hoping what she thought could be happening was just her paranoia. But as she looked down the hallway, she saw Cordell wrapping his arms around a fleeing cell guard. With one quick violent motion, the Maniac Cop then pulled his arms in opposite directions, ripping the officer's body in two at the waist. He then dropped the two parts to the floor. A bloody act done with incredible ease.

Cordell then turned on the other guard, who was crouched by the wall and couldn't bear to face what was about to happen to them. In desperation, they turned their own gun on themselves and pulled the trigger, ending their potential horror in a moment.

This, however, only seemed to enrage Cordell further. He strode over to the fallen officer, grabbed them by the legs, lifted then slammed their lifeless body down onto the floor tiles. Lifting them, then slamming them back down . . . again and again.

Through the doorway, Susan stared helplessly, and behind her, Turkell could also see.

"I knew it! You wouldn't leave me here!"

Soon the other inmates from the cells started to shout as well. Realizing that their escape could be near.

"Let me out!"

"Can I come?"

"Open the fucking cell, please!"

Susan backed up from the double doors as Cordell marched toward her. Before he walked through, he bent down to one of the guards and ripped the ring of keys from their belt.

Backing up to a nearby wall, Susan struggled to not panic. As Cordell walked into the cell area and saw her, she almost screamed. Yet he didn't come after her. He just turned back toward the cell in front of him. The cell where he had heard a voice call to him. But he could recognize the man in front of him. Instead, it was only someone covered in bandages. Cordell tilted his head in confusion.

"Cordell, I got a surprise for you." Turkell grinned. "Are you ready?" Without waiting another moment, Turkell's hand shot up and grabbed at his bandages. "You're gonna lose your shit, my brother." Finding the end of the dressing, he started to speedily unraveling the wrapping over his head. "You'll see how much I believe in you."

Nearing the end, the padding and bandages were stuck to his healing wounds. Without any gentle touch or care not to hurt his injuries further, Turkell ripped the last of the dressings off, exposing his lacerated face, ruined eye, and missing nose. As the gauze was pulled, it took off with it some of the scabbing, opening up parts of the wounds, sending fresh drippings of blood out and down onto the floor.

Cordell stood, silently staring, with a growing snarl on his face.

"Well," Turkell said, motioning to his face. "What'dya think? We're totally brothers now."

Susan watched from the wall. She could not fathom how anyone could willingly do what Turkell did to their own face. In all her years in psychology, she had not even read a case study where someone was in such a deluded state yet was still quite present in reality. She peered around the room for an escape, for a back exit. Though, she knew full well that if she moved, Cordell could and probably would decide to stop her. Then again, he didn't come after her.

Maybe he didn't recognize me? she pondered.

Cordell stared at Turkell, then looked at the other cells. At the other convict.

Turkell's smile faltered. "Hello?" he said, realizing that Cordell's attention was not on him any more.

Cordell did not know why he was here. He just knew he had to come here but did not know why. He then realized that, as Turkell spoke to him, not all of the words were aloud. They were somehow straight in his mind.

It's me, your buddy! Turkell thought, which Cordell heard.

In the whirl of fury and pain in his head, Cordell threw the bunch of keys he took from the guard into the cell at Turkell's feet. He then turned to the administration desk and began rifling through the paperwork.

Turkell quickly scurried to the keys on the floor, picked them up, and moved to the door, eager to let himself out. "I could hear what you did to the cops. Oh, man, I would have loved to have seen that happen!"

Why am I here? Turkell then heard. A guttural voice. But one that made him look at Cordell, who was still rifling through the desk, unable to have said that. But Turkell *knew* he heard it. Just as he heard many things the Maniac Cop said to him without a voice.

They were connected somehow. Connected by some malevolence.

Finding the right key, the lock released on Turkell's cell door, clinking loudly. He stepped out, ignoring the severe pain in his face as well as the blood dripping out onto his clothes. He then turned to the other cells.

"Hey, guys, want to be liberated?" He looked squarely at Blum who was out of bed and standing by his locked door. "See?" Turkell continued. "I told you to treat me nice. You thought I was a nut job, right?"

"We all got caught," Blum replied. "We're all nut jobs."

Turkell then unlocked the run of cell doors, and one by one, the prisoners stepped out. But none of them whooped or hollered. They were all too confused by what was happening and who this goliath of a cop was.

One of the prisoners, a man in his seventies, refused to even get out of his bed.

"What's with you?" Turkell asked, motioning for the man to leave the open cell. "I'm offering you freedom."

The old man motioned to Cordell, who was still looking through papers. "I don't like that guy," he said. "And I don't much like you. I'll take my chances here."

Turkell shrugged with a smile, then shut the cell door and locked it again. "Have it your way, asshole," he chuckled.

Susan couldn't just let all these men go free with Cordell. They may be people who broke the law, but no one deserved what he no doubt offered. Death.

"You're the smart one," she said aloud to the old man, which caught everyone's attention, except Cordell, who didn't react at all. She stared at the wailing escapees. "That guy's the Maniac Cop from the news. He's gonna get you all killed. He's a monster!"

Blum shrugged. "I was gonna be thrown in Sing Sing till they threw the switch on me."

"They don't have the death penalty in Sing Sing, numb nuts," another prisoner corrected. "Last one was in the sixties."

Flicking through the stacks of papers and official documents on the desk, Cordell stopped at one form. A form in triplicate. Picking it up, he read it and let out a grunt. He then crossed over back to Turkell and handed him the document, pointing to one part of the paper.

Turkell read it, and as he did, he smiled. Understanding what was happening.

Outside 1 Police Plaza, dozens of policemen stood waiting for their orders. Each of these men and women wore riot gear, complete with bullet-proof vests, helmets with large visors and large batons. Others without shields carried guns. Not just pistols but also semi-automatic rifles. They were all tooled up for a major confrontation.

Normally, in these numbers, with these weapons, they would be facing off against a huge crowd of violent protestors, not just one man. And that made everyone here even more nervous. None of them knew the truth about Matthew Cordell. All they knew was that the cops that escaped said a huge man in a police uniform had started killing everyone, and no bullet seemed to take him down. Many took this to mean that he had some advanced armor, others that there was probably a hallucinogen toxin in the air, but all of them felt a palpable fear that they were waiting for their own deaths and knew this was the Maniac Cop who decimated the St Patrick's Day parade two years before.

Detective Lovejoy stood at the far side of the parking lot, in a state of shock and bewilderment. He had gotten out of there but could not believe what he had seen. *Who* he had seen. The bullets the policemen pumped into Cordell should have been enough to stop a hundred men, but it couldn't even stop one.

"Hey, Lovejoy," McKinney called out as he walked his way past the other officers to him. "What the hell happened in there? What is all this?"

"He killed so many." Lovejoy's words were sporadic and stuttered. "I-I don't know how many he killed upstairs. We just got out of his way." He then turned to McKinney and, for the first time, addressed him by his first name. "Sean?"

McKinney was genuinely shocked at this. He hadn't been called that by anyone for many years.

"He wasn't human," Lovejoy continued. "We shot him so many times. The bullets just went through him. He's dead. He's the walking goddamn dead!"

"You got out of there. You're alive," McKinney said, trying to calm him. "That's all you need to concern yourself about." He motioned to the crowd of policemen. "These guys here will sort this out. You go. Go home. Be safe."

"Before we all got out, one of the officers had eyes on the cell block. He said that Susan Riley's been taken hostage down there."

"Hostage? Is she hurt?"

Lovejoy shrugged helplessly. "We've got the squads ready to go in. Commissioner Doyle's been notified. He said we gotta wait till he takes charge."

McKinney shook his head. "I think this is a mistake. All these cops. If only half of what you say about this guy is true, then this won't do shit to stop him."

"So, what *should* we do?"

"If he tries to get out, we shouldn't interfere. We should just follow him." He paused for a beat. "He had a reason for coming here, right? He's gotta have a reason for everything he does."

"He had to have come for Turkell."

"But why him? Cordell is a cop on a revenge trip, Turkell is a grubby little rapist serial killer. Not much common ground there, is there?"

Lovejoy turned and noticed the chief of police, Tom O'Hanlon. "We should go talk to the chief before Doyle gets here. Tell him your thoughts."

In the cell block, the bodies of two policemen had been stripped of their uniforms. Still stuck with her back to the wall, Susan stared at Turkell as he began to remove his trousers to get dressed into one of the uniforms. Something that he soon noticed.

"Hey, lady, close your eyes," he laughed. "You might see something you like."

As Turkell got dressed in the bloodstained blues, complete with eight-point hat, Blum followed suit but before he could put on the first piece of clothing, Cordell strode over and snatched the uniform out of his hands.

"What the hell, dude? How come not me?" Blum

complained, turning to Turkell as he was getting no reply from Cordell. "What's happening? Why can't I get dressed as a cop? And why doesn't he talk? It's weird. *He's* weird. You're all fucking weird."

Cordell stared down emotionlessly, and Blum could not help but stare back. He looked not only the damage to the large man's face but the new holes that were scattered all over it. They were fresh holes from bullet hits. But there was no blood. No gore. Just holes.

It made Blum feel a terrible shiver. "What are you?" he asked under his breath.

Turkell, meanwhile, held up the paperwork Cordell had handed to him. "Hey, these are your transfer papers to Sing Sing, yeah?"

"What about it? Who cares?" Blum retorted. "I'm not going there now, so they can burn."

"There's a reason you can't wear a uniform, you know?" Turkell laughed with a cocky smile. "I think what my friend here has in mind, needs you to go there. He wants to go to Sing Sing, and you're our way in."

"What?" Blum gasped. "Those bastards'll shoot me on sight. Fuck that shit!"

"He won't let that happen," Turkell said. "You've seen what he can do. No one can stop him. *No one.* You can't stop evil."

"Why there? What's in Sing Sing?" Susan asked nervously, chiding herself, afraid of the attention she brought on herself.

"Haven't you got it figured out yet, lady?" Turkell said, crossing over to stand next to Cordell. "We're going to break the guys out. There must be hundreds who'll join us. Real *lovable* types, too." He looked up at Cordell as he spoke. "We're recruiting an army, aren't we, my friend? That's what this is about." A look of almost spiritual joy came over him as he stared up at the Maniac Cop with a childlike wonder. "Your thoughts are in my head. I got you all figured out." He turned to the other convicts in the room. "See, we're not running away, we're getting stronger. We got ourselves a leader!"

One convict sucked his teeth loudly. "I don't want no part of this bullshit. I'm not going in no pen. Not for you or him. Not even Allah himself could—"

In one fluid and sudden movement, the Maniac Cop grabbed his billy club from his belt, spun it once around his hand by the strap, then lashed out toward the dissenting convict. Striking him across the neck, breaking it with one almighty blow. The cracking of the bones reverberated so loud in this room it made almost everyone wince. But not Turkell, who stared with joy. The unfortunate convict clattered to the floor in a dead heap. One less recruit but a fitting lesson to the others that there would be no argument without extreme punishment.

Turkell looked up at Cordell, then motioned with his head to Susan. "Should we bring her along as well?" he whispered.

175

Cordell nodded. Slight and almost imperceptible, but Turkell saw and understood. No one else could see this, though.

As he turned, Turkell grinned to Susan, but as he did that, he felt a slight dizziness. His injuries were still bleeding, his face afire with agonized nerve endings. *He had to focus. He had to keep on.*

"Alright, honey," he said, pointing to the doorway. "Lead the way. If there's any shooting, you'll know it before we do."

The Maniac Cop, though, moved across the room in a different direction, leading to the corridor toward the rear entrance of the building. Noticing, Turkell immediately changed direction.

"You're right, my friend," he said, answering Cordell's voice in his head. "That is a much better way to go."

The rear of the building was much like the front, encircled by cops in riot gear, each holding a range of weapons from batons to pistols to machine guns. This car park also was where all of the police vehicles were parked. The squad cars, vans, and prison transport buses.

Commissioner Doyle, having arrived in his stretched limousine, stood at the back of the cops with a look of anger. He stood alongside Tom O'Hanlon and McKinney.

"Eyes on the inside confirm they have a hostage," O'Hanlon said. "Susan Riley."

Doyle motioned to the building. ". . . And they're definitely coming out the back?"

McKinney nodded. "SWAT just confirmed it. They're not even hiding. They're just getting her to lead the way."

"I should have fired her after the television show," Doyle rued. "Then, we wouldn't be in the shit. What the hell was she doing here at this hour, anyway? Could she be a part of this?"

"Not even a little bit," McKinney replied.

Then the back doors of the building swung open loudly, and the group of seven, led by their shield, Susan, walked out. Each one of the men were holding guns they had just stolen from fallen policemen inside. And each one of these escaped convicts wore a mean expression, but they all felt the same way inside. That this was way out of their depth.

Standing behind Susan was Matthew Cordell. The officers outside the building collectively gasped as they saw him. Saw his mauled face. Then next to him was Turkell, with his fresh injuries. It was a terrible vision of violence almost too surreal to comprehend.

Susan was so close to Cordell she could smell his rotten stench. Even out here in the fresh air, his pungent smell was overpowering. "Why are you really taking them back there?" she asked, not convinced by anything Turkell had said.

Cordell did not reply.

As he walked them toward the bus, the commissioner, behind the line of armed cops, was not impressed.

"And we're just letting than all go, just like that?"

The captain nodded. "McKinney's right, Commissioner. This could be a lot bigger than just these men. We need to see where they're going and at all costs protect the hostage."

"We could just mow them all down in a hail of bullets and be done with it," Doyle grumbled. "One extra casualty of ours isn't such bad odds."

"If that is your command, then let me know. I need you to say it clearly," O'Hanlon replied. "If it goes south—which both McKinney and I say it will—then this will be on you. We will obey your command, but it will have to be yours and only yours."

Doyle didn't reply. He was stuck in indecision. He watched as the men led Susan onto one of the prison transport buses. Turkell was the last on the bus and got behind the steering wheel, immediately starting the engine.

The line of surrounding officers had no option but to part in order to let the bus through.

Right then, Doyle's nerves got the best of him. "Fire! Fire now! Get them all!" he suddenly screamed.

"No!" McKinney pleaded angrily, but it was too late.

As the bus roared out of the parking lot, the

policemen obeyed their sudden order and lifted their guns.

The convicts in the back of the bus saw this and immediately lifted their own weapons. A sudden cross-fire of lead filled the parking lot as the bus drove away. Most of its windows shattered as soon as the bullets started to fly.

Cordell was sitting beside Turkell, and both were sprayed in glass from the shattering windshield in front of them but neither moved nor were hurt by any of the flying shards. Nor were Susan or Blum, who sat a few rows back. But for the three other escaped convicts at the back of the bus . . . they were not so lucky. The bullets had split through the chassis, littering the back seats with holes. The convicts who chose to sit there had no chance.

At the junction ahead, police cars moved forward to block the street, block their escape. But the bus was not intimidated nor was it even slowing down. The large vehicle crashed through the police cruisers with ease, overturning them with the policemen still inside. Plowing through and driving away as both police cars burst into flames. The police inside burning alive with tormented cries for help.

Back at the station, McKinney was incensed by what happened. He glared in anger at the commissioner, who just looked back at him with a shrug.

"What?" Doyle said. "We *have* to stop them. We got no choice!"

"She better not be hurt," McKinney threatened. "She's one of us!"

"And so was Cordell," O'Hanlon added, also not looking impressed with the commissioners sudden ruling.

"Don't mention that name!" Doyle hissed back. "It can't be him. It can't! He's *dead*."

"Oh, I know you think that," McKinney said, having had enough. "But you fucking saw him, right there!" he shouted, pointing to the station. "Who else d'ya think it was? Santa fucking Claus? Huh? No. And I know why you're saying it's not him. 'Cause if it is, then you got a shit load to answer for, don't you?"

Down the dark city streets, the bus raced at its maximum speed. Turkell was joyous as he gripped the wheel, focused on the escape.

Behind, Susan looked frightened, while, across from her, Blum stared at her with an unsettling, lasciviously gaze. He never had thought that after being sentenced to life that he would be able to see a woman again, let alone get what he wanted from one. With his gun firmly in his grip, he reached out across the seat and stroked her hair with the barrel.

She immediately recoiled in disgust.

"You're too good-looking to be a cop, you know that?" he said with a sickly glee. "Why don't you hike that skirt up a bit higher, so I can see your legs better or even higher, so I can see . . . more."

She didn't move a muscle.

His glee turned into an immediate grimace. "You heard me, cunt. Moved it *all* the way up. I wanna see everything you got. *RIGHT NOW!*"

She wanted to scream, but he had a gun, and she could not take her eyes off it, He started to hold it toward her threateningly.

Click.

Susan winced. But the sound did not come from Blum's gun. Both of them turned in surprise and saw the revolver pointed right at Blum's head. A revolver held by Cordell, which immediately stopped Blum in his tracks.

Though the Maniac Cop didn't speak, he did not need to. Blum got the message. He was not to touch her.

Relieved and somehow grateful to the deranged Cordell, Susan got up out of her seat and walked to the front of the bus. Away from Blum.

The wind from outside blustered in hard as the bus sped along, onto the northbound Saw Mill River Parkway, toward Ossining. Toward Sing Sing Penitentiary.

"Why did you stop him?" Susan asked Cordell, sitting in the seat behind him. "Why do you care what happens to me?"

The Maniac Cop did not turn or respond.

She stared at him, confused by him and by everything.

"What do you mean you fucking lost him?" Doyle shouted at the unfortunate officer, who had just given update that the pursuit cars had all been rammed off the streets by the bus. "This is a PR nightmare!"

McKinney had had enough of the commissioner and was talking to the chief of police, with a few other members of his team.

"We found Cordell's car," McKinney said. "Just parked up on Oliver street. He must have jacked it from the compound. Was an old issue cruiser."

"My guess, like the one he used to drive?" O'Hanlon suggested.

"Probably. Anyway, somehow, the smart assholes didn't deactivate the police radio in it. So, that's how he has known everything about this. How he knew Turkell was here. This is a plan, I know it, but I can't, for the life of me, figure out what the hell it is."

O'Hanlon looked out toward the exit the bus went. "The big problem we have is that we are trying to put sanity into insanity. Logic may not apply here. It may be all luck."

McKinney thought for a second. "Where could they be going?"

Right then, as he said that, something clicked. A lot

of things clicked. He suddenly saw a much bigger picture.

Out of his periphery, McKinney noticed Doyle walking away toward his driver, who was standing by obediently. "Hey, Doyle," he called out. "Let me give you a ride."

Doyle waved his hand dismissively. "I got a ride, Detective."

"We *have* to talk," McKinney said sternly. "If you wanna survive this with your life intact, you better listen . . ." He paused. "I know what you did."

Considering the options for a moment, Doyle turned to his driver. "You can go."

In his car, McKinney pulled away with the commissioner in the passenger seat.

"So," Doyle asked, "you gonna tell me what's so damn important that you gotta threaten me?"

"It's not my threats, but you're the only one who can stop this."

Doyle looked confused, then at the direction they were going. "Wait, where are you driving? This isn't toward the city. This goes to the parkway."

"I know the route they took," McKinney said, pressing harder on the accelerator. "I know where he's going."

"What the hell?" Doyle cried out in annoyance. "Why didn't you say so? We have units being corralled

Christian Francis

all over goddamn Manhattan. If you know where he's going, we have to get everyone there. Every cop. Every gun—"

"All the cops in the world can't stop him," McKinney interrupted.

"Oh, and you think I can?" Doyle was stunned. "And how would that be done, exactly? Me going mano a mano against that thing?"

McKinney shook his head.

Doyle was incensed. "Stop this car. I'm getting out! That's an order."

But McKinney didn't slow down. He just went faster. And as he did, he wound down the window and placed his police light onto the roof.

Doyle looked slightly panicked.

"What got me was that Turkell thing," McKinney said. "Why the hell would a cop, even one like Cordell, want to be with him? Then I realized something. It's a long con. He's been listening in on us. Misdirecting us. Pulling our attention away from the one thing we would not think of doing."

"What's that then o' wise sage?" Doyle asked sarcastically.

"I don't think he was there for Turkell. I think he was there for a prisoner. All cops know that our cells hold people on their way to Sing Sing. And even with his size, he can't just break into it. It's too well guarded. You can't punch your way past all that steel and brick. He needs to get in some other way."

184

Doyle didn't buy it. "So, he was just gonna walk up with a prisoner to open the gate? With his face? No one would let him in . . ." As he said those words, realization came. "Oh . . . Stephen Turkell."

McKinney nodded. "It's a theory. A long shot. But it makes sense."

"But he butchered himself. The guards would see that."

"I don't think Turkell has anything to do with this," McKinney said softly. "It's Susan Riley. He's took her, too. She's not uniform, but she's still a cop."

"So, why did he take Turkell in the first place?"

"Maybe he was plan A? Maybe a distraction? Either way, there is only one way to know for sure."

Doyle thought for a moment. "And how can I stop Cordell when a dozen bullets didn't?"

"Oh, you finally believe in ghosts?" McKinney smirked, glancing to Doyle. "You ought to. You made him one!"

Doyle sneered. He never wanted to hear the name Cordell again.

"I heard a lot of shit in my years," McKinney continued. "And I knew a lot of old boys who knew Cordell. Worked with him. He was City Hall's guard dog. Doing the dirty work for them. Doing what he was ordered. Everyone knew that. Then he was suddenly in the spotlight as a dirty cop. Now, I didn't get why. City Hall could have blamed anyone, but they blamed *him*. So, I looked into it, and the one person who had to have known what was happening was the captain at the time. So, tell me. What the fuck did you do to him?"

Doyle suddenly pulled his revolver from his holster and pointed it at McKinney. "Turn this damn car around!"

McKinney was not intimidated, nor did he change course. "Now that's a dumb fucking thing to do, commissioner."

"What do you expect? Me to hand myself over to that *thing*? Let him murder me, too? What, 'cause I did what I was told? Sure, he went down, but he still killed a lot of people without due process. The charges were not faked."

"People *you* ordered him to kill."

Doyle did not answer. He was trying to think of a way out of it.

"The only thing I can think of is that he saw something he shouldn't have. 'Cause you all turned on him where there was no investigation or public inquiry. You all just turned. Why?"

"What can I do to fix this?" Doyle said, averting the subject.

"What can you do? You can make it good, that's what . . . You reopen the Cordell case. Get some judge to set aside his conviction. Blame it all on your predecessor if you have to. You can save yourself and still do the right thing. Then dig up his empty coffin, 'cause you know it is definitely empty, then bury it again with a police honor guard. *That's* how you stop this. He's after revenge. So, you gotta make it as right as you can. Then he will have nothing left to get revenge for. If he's not a monster, he won't act a monster. But you made him a monster!"

"That's insane. You have no idea that'll work, and even if it could—"

McKinney said, his contempt at the forefront of his tone, "Even if I *don't* know the details, I know that you all sacrificed him to get away with whatever the fuck you were all doing. Maybe you weren't in charge, but you went along with it."

"You're pushing me too far, McKinney!" Doyle said as he pushed his revolver nearer.

Having enough, McKinney slammed on the brakes, knocking Doyle forward into the dashboard. With one hand, he easily disarmed the commissioner, who had not even fired a gun for well over a decade.

Dazed and confused, Doyle held his head. "Fine," he shouted, his head ringing from the impact. "But what the hell power do I have to do all that?"

"Oh, it's not just that. You gotta sign a confession and name all the people involved."

"What? I'd be through if I do that!"

McKinney turned and pointed the commissioner's own gun at him. "No offense, but after what you did in this car, you're through anyway. And even without me, he will probably come after you if you don't stop him. Kill you, your family. All for what? 'Cause of you

Christian Francis

hiding the shit you did? Setting things right means you all owning up to this."

"How do you even know any of this will work?"

"Work? I don't know it'll work, but it's the only chance you have. And if it doesn't work, you'll have still done something to fix a past mistake."

Even back in 1976, Doyle knew this would all come back to haunt them. Until that, he had no belief that Cordell could have been really back. He had managed to convince himself it was everyone else who was deluded, and they were just all mistaken. But when he saw the Maniac Cop exiting the police station, he finally saw the truth.

Doyle knew that every word McKinney just said was right. And if McKinney can piece together what happened, anyone could. If he did nothing and Cordell didn't come after him, people could still find out. And he knew for damn sure McKinney would not keep that secret.

Cordell had already come back to kill people involved in his death. And McKinney knew that every order came through Doyle. Every hit to a criminal who they didn't have enough evidence to convict was from his mouth. The money that disappeared from the crime scenes was arranged by him. Cordell may have done bad things, but he was doing them because Doyle and his superiors convinced him that it was the right thing to do and that he would be protected. But it was the money that turned him. When he found out that

188

money was being taken and spread among Doyle and the others, Cordell threatened them. So, they did what they did. Rooke, Pike, and Doyle.

Doyle sank in the seat as he realized it was all over. "All right . . . I'll do it. I'll sort this out . . . And if it doesn't work, then . . . Then at least . . . At least I won't have it on my conscience anymore."

McKinney nodded and picked up the radio mic. "Central, Commissioner Doyle for the mayor," he said. "Patch me through. It's urgent. It concerns the massacre at 1 Police Plaza."

Chapter 9

The nighttime was getting old as the bus pulled off the parkway, passing the signpost that pointed them to the state penitentiary.

Turkell, still behind the wheel, was in a constant state of giggling. Half from his loose grip on sanity, the other from the delirium of the injuries on his face. Already, the blood had started to scab once more as the wind blew in through the shattered windshield, drying out the injuries to the point where even smiling caused pain. But he didn't care. He was past all that.

"This is the last place they'd expect us to go," he gleefully mumbled as ahead the large gates to Sing Sing lay ahead.

In the guard room of the penitentiary, the officer on duty glanced at the CCTV monitor, at the black-and-white image of the police prisoner transport pulling up. Through the screen, the damage on the bus could not be seen nor could the injuries over Turkell's face. All the guard could see was the bus, the number plate, and the person exiting the vehicle wearing a police uniform, with an eight-point hat on.

That person on the screen walked over to an intercom on a post by the main doors. "Delivering the prisoner, Blum, Joseph T.," the man said, pressing the call button.

Leaning forward, the guard spoke into his mic. "Weren't expecting you till morning. What's the rush?"

Outside, Turkell had his back to the camera and was into the intercom. "We got a tip. His friends might create some problems for us. So, we played it safe." As he spoke, he glanced back to the bus, to Cordell.

"Don't blame ya," the guard replied. His voice almost lost among the static noise on the speaker. "Hand the transfer papers to the guard when inside, okay?"

"Ten-four, good buddy," Turkell said, letting go of the intercom button and walking back to the bus.

Getting back behind the wheel, the buzzer to the prison doors sounded, the loud electric thrum that signaled that the metal entrance doors were about to open.

Driving through the gates, the bus drove into a courtyard where a second security gate in front of them stood. As the gate behind them closed, this one soon opened.

As they drove through, they entered Sing Sing's main courtyard.

The captain of the guards paid their arrival little mind as did the centuries up in the towers overlooking the courtyard. They just saw a police vehicle, then a prisoner being led out. The same thing they saw dozens of times a day. Nothing to dwell on.

Up front, Turkell had a grip on Blum's arm, with him apparently handcuffed with his hands behind his body. He was led to the main building, and his face looked nervous. Unlike the rest of what they were doing, this was not an act. Blum did not want to be here but also did not want to suffer the wrath of the Maniac Cop.

Turkell's head was lowered, hiding his face behind the peak of his hat. Behind them, Cordell and Susan followed.

Susan kept looking up at Cordell. She did not know why, but she felt some pity for him. She knew the unforgivable things he had done, even to her, but still felt a great sadness about him. A torment that drove him. That there was something more than the killing machine that he showed. She stared at his face and the bullet holes. She knew from her stomach to her heart that this man was not living. He was a zombie. He had to be. Nothing could live after that much done to them. And he was so cold and reeked of death. *The deaf policeman heard the noise. Came and shot the two dead boys*, she thought again to herself.

Just then, she looked at Turkell, then back to Cordell and remembered something she was told as a kid in Hebrew school about a golem. *Could this be . . . ?* She had to shake off all her theories. She had to concern herself more about getting out of there. What-ever the reason they brought her, she could not dwindle on questions that would not help her fate.

As the group proceeded toward the main cell block door, it was already in the process of being unlocked by the security personnel, all of whom still paid little attention to any of the new arrivals.

It was an older prison trustee, an inmate who had earned special privileges, who looked at them for longer than a brief glance. Ignacio Ruiz, an ex-gang boss who, nowadays, just kept his head down and served his time, stared in horror. He had pulled a late duty and had been rolling out the trash carts from the kitchen block when he saw them. When he saw the large mutilated cop. The cop he recognized.

His face fell. "No," he whispered. "That's not possible." His breathing stuttered as the word trembled off his lips. "Cordell."

He was the man who held one of the blades long

ago. He was the one who slashed Cordell's nose from his face. He had never seen Cordell in uniform but knew how the man looked after they had finished with him all those years ago. Those scars were extreme and unmistakable.

Immediately, he turned and rushed back inside the prison building, leaving the trash cart where it was.

In the guard tower, the captain of the guards was on the phone. "Yes Warden," he said. "That inmate has just been delivered through the gates."

"What do you mean he's there?" The warden's voice rang out loudly over the phone. "I just got word that he broke out of holding with some high-profile people and had kidnapped a female officer."

"Well, I don't know what to tell you. He just arrived under heavy escort five minutes ago. He is being delivered as we speak. I really don't think he escaped."

"Heavy escort? No! They escaped on a prison transport bus." The warden's panic raised. "They're not police. Seal off the section of the cell block immediately. Put all men on alert! You just let in that goddamn maniac cop!"

Turkell walked ahead, with Blum in his grip, still playing as if he was handcuffed. Behind, Cordell and

Susan walked at a close pace. They moved toward the large set of doors leading to the main prison block. The last line of security before they got to the cells.

Ahead, two guards unlocked the doors without looking up to examine who was approaching. They just saw the prisoner and the blur of police uniforms, then opened the door wide to let them in.

As soon as the group stepped across the threshold to the inner sanctum of the prison, one of the guards looked at Turkell, ready to smile politely and ask for the transfer documentation. Instead, he was met with the bloodied and freshly carved face of an insane murderer, who smiled at him sadistically. As he did as his cheeks lifted, the dried scabbing parts of his injuries cracked open, and fresh rivulets of blood seeped out.

Letting go of Blum's arm, Turkell lunged at the guard, mouth first, toward his neck. The officer had no time to react as Turkell was on him and bit down hard on his jugular, ripping out his throat with a savage growl.

Blum headbutted the other guard, and when the man had fallen to the floor, Blum started stamping on his head repeatedly.

Susan gasped in terror and disgust, wanting to run, but as she turned, she noticed Cordell looking down at her. Watching her.

She was stuck. She could not escape. Still, she glanced around the area, looking for any way out. But she saw none.

. . .

In an adjoining building, the inmates were being led back to their cells, after a movie screening in the rec room. They were all oblivious to what was happening in the next block.

With fifteen minutes to go until late curfew, they were meandering their way back. Smoking and enjoying this break in the routine.

From one end of the block, Ignacio Ruiz, the prison trustee, ran in, still in shock from what he had seen.

"Cordell!" he said in a panic to a group of cronies waiting at the bottom of the stairs to the next level of cells. "I fucking saw *Cordell*! He's alive! He's fucking here! That program we saw . . . It wasn't lying!"

"You been huffing paint?" one chuckled as the rest joined in laughing at this.

"I'm telling you he's *alive,* and he's here. He's gotta be back to get us," Ignacio insisted, but he was just met with more derisive laughter.

"Well, fuck you all." Ignacio seethed as he turned and walked away. "I'll look out for myself, then."

They had all watched *Criminals At Large,* and when Cordell was mentioned, it did not frighten a single one of them. Those who remembered him knew he was dead. They thought this was to scare the public. No one considered any of it to be real.

Rushing to his cell, Ignacio quickly turned, making sure no guards were looking or nearby. When the coast was clear, he knelt by his toilet, reached behind, and pulled out a bunched-up sheet from between the pipes. Unwrapping them, he pulled out a shank, a lighter, and small bottle filled with stolen gasoline from the motor pool. This bottle, complete with fabric shoved into its neck, was a crude Molotov cocktail.

Back in the main cell block, in front of the cells containing many prisoners, the two guards lay dead by the open doors. One with his throat bitten out, having bled out over the floor, the other with his head stamped in from Blum's heel.

The prisoners in their cells had witnessed this and were cheering and yelling like they were watching a football match. Loving every second of the violence on display. They all cried out to be freed, wanting to join whatever this was. These inmates of this section had two things in common, they were lifers and each had committed the most violent of crimes.

Turkell smiled, his wounds cracking again. His body was weak but ran on pure mania. He was in chronic pain yet did not care. He even kind of liked how it felt.

"Okay, you guys," he called out loudly. Causing the inmates to quieten. "Hang on, I know how anxious you all are. We'll get you out, don't you worry."

From the cells, a unified cheer erupted.

"We're recruiting an army, you see?" Turkell

shouted over the noise. "And you can be part of it." He turned to Cordell, enraptured in the moment. "Right? They all can join us?"

But Cordell was making no moves. He was still. Standing next to Susan staring forward.

"Cordell?" Turkell added. His smile faltering. "What are we waiting for?"

Cordell didn't know the answer. His mind was a kaleidoscope of deafening pain. All he thought about was where he was, and that filled him with even more rage than he had felt in a long time.

From the PA speakers on the walls, a click sounded, followed by a voice. A voice that caused everyone to stop what they were doing and pay attention. It was loud, almost too loud. The sound sharp and booming.

"Attention. This police commissioner, Edward Doyle. I'm talking to Officer Matthew Cordell," the voice rang out.

Cordell know that voice well. His attention turned to the nearest speaker as his fists clenched tightly.

"Cordell? If you are listening . . ." Doyle continued sounding nervous. "I can confirm that Judge Arthur Claypool has ordered your trial immediately reopened . . . at my request."

Turkell's smile was completely gone as he turned to the Maniac Cop with a perturbed confusion. "Cordell? What the fuck do you need a new trial for? Who is that guy?"

Susan could not keep silent. She had to speak, risking her life among these murders. "Matthew," she said, trying to connect to the man inside the beast, "this is what you wanted, didn't you? Justice?"

Turkell shot her a look of fury.

In the courtyard outside, Doyle was holding a remote microphone, shifting from side to side as he glanced at McKinney.

"Keep talking," the detective urged.

Doyle's gaze crossed to the guards and warden, who stood close by, all looking confused at the night's events.

He continued into the microphone. "In your first trial, perjury was committed," he said as his voice wavered. "Even the presiding judge was influenced. You were not the guilty one. They were . . ." he paused for a second. "I-I was . . ." He closed his eyes in shame. Behind him, the warden and guards looked in shock.

"Matthew Cordell was a good man," Doyle said. "He was a good cop. He did not deserve a thing that happened to him."

McKinney was surprised. Surprised that this man would ever admit to what he did wrong. He thought for sure that he would just blame it all on everyone else involved. But instead, he crumbled immediately and was here, unburdening his guilt in public. McKinney could not help but feel for the guy, even if he deserved it.

"A good fucking cop?" Turkell screamed at Cordell. "What the fuck is he talking about?"

Cordell was not listening. He turned and moved away from the cells in front of him, toward the corridor leading to the adjacent cell block. Everyone in their cells started to jeer and yell again, this time in anger, as they watched the Maniac Cop walk away. They heard what was said, too, and none of them were happy about it. Blum had no idea what to say or do as he just stared at the incensed Turkell.

Susan, not knowing what she could do, started to follow Cordell.

"Cordell," the commissioner continued over the PA. "Your conviction and sentence will be reversed by the state supreme court. I can assure you of that. I will see to it that the truth comes out. That everything is set right. Please stop what you are doing. You don't need any more revenge."

"You can't leave us here," Turkell screamed as he raced after Cordell, Blum following suit. "Tell us what to do. We had a deal. We're brothers!" He motioned to his face. "Look what I did for you!"

· · ·

In the next block on the second floor, Ignacio stood in his dark cell, Molotov and shank in hand. None of the barred doors had been closed yet. The guards had all been distracted by what came over the PA speakers, as were the inmates. All had listened to the commissioner's confession and heard the name Cordell.

"I'm ready for you," Ignacio muttered, stepping forward into the corridor, his voice trembling. "I killed you once. I can do it again."

A red light on the wall flicked on as a harsh buzzer sounded. The call for emergency lock down.

The guards were suddenly alerted. They needed to get everyone in their cells immediately.

"Okay, back it up. Fun's all over!" one guard shouted. "Back it up in your cells, *now!*"

Suddenly, the huge metal door at the end of the tiered cellblock began to rattle and shake. A loud clanking of metal on metal as the entrance was ripped off its hinges by an incredible force.

Now on the walkway, Ignacio Ruiz, with weapons in his hands, jolted at the noise. He could not see what was coming, but he *knew* what it was. He had a deep feeling of dread. He *knew* it was Cordell. He did not know why he was here, but he could only think it was for the same thing that he would be after if he were in Cordell's shoes: revenge against those who wronged him. And if that *was* Cordell coming in now, then Ignacio would do his best to survive.

There were others in this block who were in that

shower room that night. He wasn't the only one who had attacked Cordell. This was after all the block Cordell had been put in all those years ago. Over half of those in these cells were here in '76. They remembered all too well that giant of a man, the disgraced cop, being sent down with them. Him being the one that put most of them away in the first place.

Back then, Ignacio had been a kingpin in this block, but over the following decade, his position had been usurped for a younger, tougher guy. He was cast out of the gang and was just another inmate. He was due for release in 2001, and with his Molotov cocktail in one hand, shank in the other, all Ignacio wanted was to make sure he lived long enough to smell that freedom once again.

Around the block, panicked gasps could be heard from the inmates who saw Matthew Cordell striding in. Various people saw him and knew who it was, even if they couldn't believe it. It may have been a decade since they last saw the man but the cuts over his face, the missing nose, the police uniform. Those who were part of his demise knew how they left his body. Over half a dozen of those men were still on the block, and for those that weren't, they had heard the rumors from the television. And when one inmate gasped, "It's Cordell!" in a loud voice, it sent a shockwave of panic

Christian Francis

throughout guards and inmates alike as they all backed away.

Cordell's uniform was bloodied, dirty, moldy, riddled in bullet holes, and his face for the first time conveyed and emotion, anger. His mutilated features all contorted into a animalistic snarl.

He had no time to attack anyone before Ignacio had run to the edge of the balcony, lit his Molotov cocktail and hurled it down upon him.

On impact, the flaming bottle exploded and covered Cordell from his feet to his hat. Igniting him into a living torch. Any normal person would have fallen to the floor in agony as the flames bit at them, but Cordell did not even seem to care.

Prisoners tried to get out of his path as others tried to attack him. With their homemade weapons, a slash, a cut a thump, none did any damage. But for each person that came close enough, they were grabbed by the flaming man, crunched under his grip, then hurled across the room or onto the upper tier. One by one, he smashed, then cast aside those who battled him. There was no mercy.

Guards drew their weapons and fired at him but as with all the bullets he had taken, they had no effect. Then, if Cordell got to the ones firing at him, they, too, suffered the same deathly fate he visited upon anyone else in his path.

· · ·

In the courtyard, Doyle looked devastated as he still spoke into the microphone. "I'll be signing a confession about my part in this," he said. "I'm guilty. Do you hear me? I'll make sure the truth is told. I . . . I'm sorry Cordell. I am. You deserved better. So, please. Stop this madness. It's over."

McKinney stepped up. "It's the right thing to do," he said. "And he has to have heard it."

"What now?" Doyle asked.

"I guess it's over to me." McKinney replied as he turned to the warden. "Can you get me into the cell block?"

"Only safe, easy way in is through the heating ducts," the warden said. "You can't get out that way, though. If you go in through there, you can only come out the front doors."

Cordell made his way through the cells and headed toward the stairs leading to the fourth floor, to the shower block. On his way, he murdered anyone who he caught. Without a care for who they were, he saw them as those who did him wrong. In his rotten mind the events of his demise played on repeat as they always did, the blades, the punches, the hits. Each attempt of his to fight back eventually failing, then him being murdered as the shower water rained down upon him.

As he stepped into the same room where he was murdered, he was on fire. His uniform was being burned away and crusted into his skin as his dead flesh blistered.

The prisoners and guards that had escaped him so far were backed up into the expansive shower block. And as he walked in, convict or guard, if he got them, he pummeled, ripped and tore them asunder.

Susan had walked in behind Cordell to the cell block, but as the fury ensured, Turkell and Blum were on her and grabbed hold of her making sure she couldn't escape.

As Turkell trailed in, avoiding any gunfire, he had seen Cordell's billy club lying on the floor. Dropped by accident from one of the maniac cops many bloody brawls.

Speedily, he grabbed it and carried on toward the shower block. Behind him, Blum held Susan tighter. She was his hostage and most likely his only ticket out of there.

Running past dozens of dead or dying prisoners and guards, Turkell kept low as he moved closer to the showers block. As he did, he could hear was the pained cries and screams of those who tried and failed to get away from the Maniac Cop.

When he got to the block, Turkell saw the still aflame Cordell confront prisoner. With shank in hand, the prisoner was frantically slashing at his attacker, trying to keep him away. But his attempts did not work. Cordell simply reached out, grabbed the man by the throat, and lifted him, ready to snap his neck.

But he then paused.

The nightmares in his mind tore into the present as he saw the prisoner in his grasp. It was Ignacio Ruiz. In his mind, Cordell had seen this man countless times. Much younger, standing in this very room, his eyes gleaming with a twisted delight as he approached with a razor. He would never forget his face.

Since entering this cell block, this was the first person Cordell had recognized from that night. The first person here he had really *seen*. Everyone before were a blur of relentless anger. They had no identity. They were just his carnage. For Ignacio, though, a simple strangulation could not enough.

With his other hand, with the flames having burned through the glove and blackened his skin, he grabbed at Ignacio's face. His powerful fingers dug into the man's eyes and curled inward. Then, with one swift movement, he yanked his hand back, breaking off the front of his face with a horrific sound. Ignacio tried to beg for forgiveness, but his jaw had been ripped away, too, and his tongue lolled outward loosely as all that sounded was a gurgled shriek.

Turkell watched this in abject horror as someone who he thought was his savior was turning against the very people they had come to save. The army he thought was being amassed. Cordell was killing his own. He had betrayed everyone.

Unscrewing the billy club he picked up, Turkell unsheathed its stiletto blade and strode over to the still burning Cordell. He raised the blade, ready to attack from behind, then paused. He could not believe it. His own missing nose, burst eye, and lacerated flesh were a testament to this man. A man he thought was his friend, his savior. "I did *everything* for you," he screamed, distraught. He then thrust the blade deep between Cordell's shoulder blades. "We were supposed to be friends," he cried.

Before Turkell could pull the blade out to stab once more, Cordell dropped the dead Ignacio to the shower room floor and turned to face his new attacker.

Turkell backed away as the flames almost licked his face, but it was not far enough. Cordell's burning hand shot out and seized him by the wrist. Immediately, the fire that covered the Maniac Cop caught onto Turkell, sweeping over him at speed.

"You were my friend!" Turkell screamed as the incineration took over.

He was not like Cordell. He was not a being that mocked death. Cordell's uniform even seemed to burn slower than it should have done. The very fabric seemed to carry the same properties as he did. It burned in places, blackened, but it did not get consumed. Turkell, on the other hand, was human. A twisted, evil human but still, he was nothing special. He could not withstand the heat of the fire. He could only scream as he was cooked alive, with Cordell still gripping his wrist, keeping him in place.

As Turkell's brain booked in his skull, Cordell felt

something. A clarity. Not much, but he felt less confused. Less in a fog.

The remaining inmates and guards were all huddled at the other end of the showers, staring in fear at what was happening. It didn't matter who they were; they were equal in Cordell's eyes and the same in their mortal fear.

At the entrance to the room, Blum was in shock, too. He still held Susan in his grip, but his eyes were locked on the scene. He stared at Cordell's murder of Turkell. He could only panic as to why he even came here. Susan, however, could not watch. She had turned away, her eyes tightly shut.

Slowly, as Turkell fell dead to the ground, still gripped by the wrist, Cordell stopped moving. In his mind, the fog of noise in his head cleared and the endless loop of his downfall dissipated. Around him reality started to bleed in. *Pain started to bleed in.* The flames over him were no longer burning ineffectually. They started to hurt as they consumed him. He tried to let go of Turkell's wrist, but his grip was fused onto the dead man by the heat.

He then turned as he saw all the death around him. He remembered doing all of this, and he was glad he did, but he could not think of what he should do now. It had all been leading here.

And then there was her.

He turned to the end of the room and looked at Susan. She was looking away, still held by Blum.

A deep, pained breath filled his ruined lungs before he let loose a loud roar, a guttural cry that tore through the room like a animal's wail. The sound snatched hers and everyone else's attention toward him, her wide eyes locked onto his monstrous form.

She expected him to run at her and Blum and kill them both.

But Cordell didn't move.

The corpses that lie around him were deserving in his mind. TAs was everyone he had decimated. Innocent or guilty of his downfall, they were to pay. And he nearly added Susan to his list.

But he saw her in the cells at 1 Police Plaza and felt no rage. He felt something else. He felt her watching him with a look other than fear. She looked at him, wanting to understand.

That's why she was here.

Not to die. Not like the others.

To witness.

Cordell had been betrayed, used, discarded by the system he once served. Every step he had taken since that day had been to not only make sure the guilty paid in blood but to make *everyone* pay in blood. To make the city pay. Man, woman, and child. But justice was meaningless if there was no one left to know why it happened, and she was the first person who looked at him wanting to know.

She would see what happened. She would remember. And when the fires finally consumed him, when his vengeance had finally run its course, she would be the one left standing.

As she stared, he began to feel weaker by the moment. He knew he was in the same room where he had died in 1976 and one thought quickly filled his decaying brain. He could not allow himself to die here again.

He looked at Susan, and with his head engulfed in torturous fire, he nodded to her. Then, dragging Turkell's corpse by the wrist, he quickly turned and broke into a sprint toward the far end of the shower block. The huddled survivors who were there, parted in a panic, scattering as the behemoth got closer.

Outside, overlooking the courtyard, the brick wall of the cell block burst outward from the fourth floor, and two figures afire came hurtling downward.

The two attached burning figures plunged toward the cement. Landing with a deafening thud. Their bodies bursting apart as they collided with the immovable ground.

The warden, guards, and commissioner recoiled in horror. Unable to speak or react as there the man lay, the Maniac Cop, burning to ashes as the flames finally broke whatever hold there had been over his afterlife.

· · ·

McKinney had witnessed it all from a heating duct that overlooked the shower rooms. He did not know what he could do, but the Maniac Cop was gone, and he saw Susan still being held by Blum and knew he had to intervene.

Dropping down onto the walkway, he quickly made his way down the steps. Blum quickly spotted him and recognized him as a detective from the station. In a panic, he quickly lifted his gun and fired. As he did, he pulled Susan in closer, holding her like a human shield.

"Fuck you, cop," he cried out angrily.

McKinney ducked behind a waist-high stone partition as the bullet narrowly missed and thudded into the tiled wall.

The other inmates and guards were all rushing out of the room. Scared more horrors could unfold.

Susan Riley, though, was no wallflower. She saw it all and knew she had a chance finally. She slammed her head backward, smashing into Blum's nose, breaking it on impact. As he loosened his group in a daze, she spun around and speedily kicked him hard in the groin. To which he fell to his knees in a hunch as he raised the gun again to her in a fury.

"*Move*," she heard McKinney shouting.

As she did, a volley of gunfire sounded, hitting Blum in the face and chest. Five shots from McKinney's gun. Each hitting their intended target.

. . .

"Today, we commend the last remains of Officer Matthew Cordell to their final resting place, alongside his brothers and sisters in service," the priest said solemnly.

In the middle of St. Raymond's Cemetery, the funeral for the man known as Matthew Cordell was being held. Not for the monster that followed but the man. It was a funeral with full honors.

The mayor stood with his head bowed in reverence as did the chief of police, Detective Lieutenant McKinney, Susan Riley and over fifty uniformed officers. No one knew what to say, how to act. No one could understand what had happened after the commissioner's confession. Gone was the blame on Cordell for the Maniac Cop killings. Instead, Stephen Turkell was named as the suspect of not just the exotic dancers but of every victim of the Maniac Cop's rampage. Everyone in the NYPD and anyone who saw the television show thought Matthew Cordell had been the killer, but they were being told something else.

Cordell's name was cleared. His reputation restored. And the press could not get enough of the story.

The priest continued. "May the mercy of the Almighty grant him peace beyond this life and may his soul, once burdened, now find eternal rest in the embrace of the Lord."

.   .   .

After the service as everyone dispersed, McKinney and Susan stood by the open grave, looking down at the casket. Nearby, a grave digger was preparing to fill in the hole.

From his pocket, McKinney pulled out a police badge, one that said Cordell on the name plate.

"Is that his?" Susan asked.

McKinney nodded. "It was found at the pier . . . I got it out of evidence. Thought he should have it." He then tossed the badge down into the hole. It clanked on the coffin lid as it landed.

Susan looked perturbed by her thoughts. "You know," she said. "Despite all the awful things. The innocent people he murdered . . . He even tried to kill me for Christ's sake . . . I can't help but feel sorry for him. Why is that?"

"He was a good cop. He did what he was told. He was used," he mused. "Yeah, he killed bad guys when he was on beat. But every time that we feel that arresting some bastard isn't enough, we all want to punish them. Stop them. Protect the innocent. We all know how just it would be to stop them. And he did that. He did that for them. For the bastards at City Hall. And they punished him out of their own cowardice." Turning from the grave, he looked at her. "He was a monster, but *they* made him one. That's why you feel bad. You have compassion."

Susan nodded sadly, knowing that whatever

Cordell was and why he did it all would forever be a mystery.

"I got some good news, though," McKinney said. "Teresa Mallory woke up. I have no idea how, but she survived."

Dirt lay heavy on the coffin as the day went on, a final seal on the nightmare that was the Maniac Cop. The silver police badge, tarnished and forgotten, lay pressed against the lid, compacted beneath six feet of cold earth. Matthew Cordell was dead and gone.

The days came and went. The months spun by taking the seasons with them. Through all of this, the grave of Matthew Cordell lay, forgotten about. No one come to place flowers on his final resting place or ever stopped to read his headstone. By the time two years had passed, the ground had slightly subsided and the grass upon it grew unkempt.

Then . . .

. . . impossibly . . .

. . . something stirred. Something called to him.

In the suffocating blackness of Matthew Cordell's coffin, charred fingers, partially skeletal, began to twitch. They flexed as bone and burned flesh cracked under the motion. Slowly, they moved, beginning to grope against the inside of the wooden casket, clawing, scraping, reaching, hungering for that badge that lay just beyond its grasp.

Outside, the day remained still. A gentle wind whispered through the cemetery, rustling the dead leaves across the grass. But beneath the gravestone of Officer Matthew Cordell, something unnatural was happening.

He had been buried. He had been burned. He had been condemned to the ground. His revenge has been sought. But something else commanded him, and he woke once more.

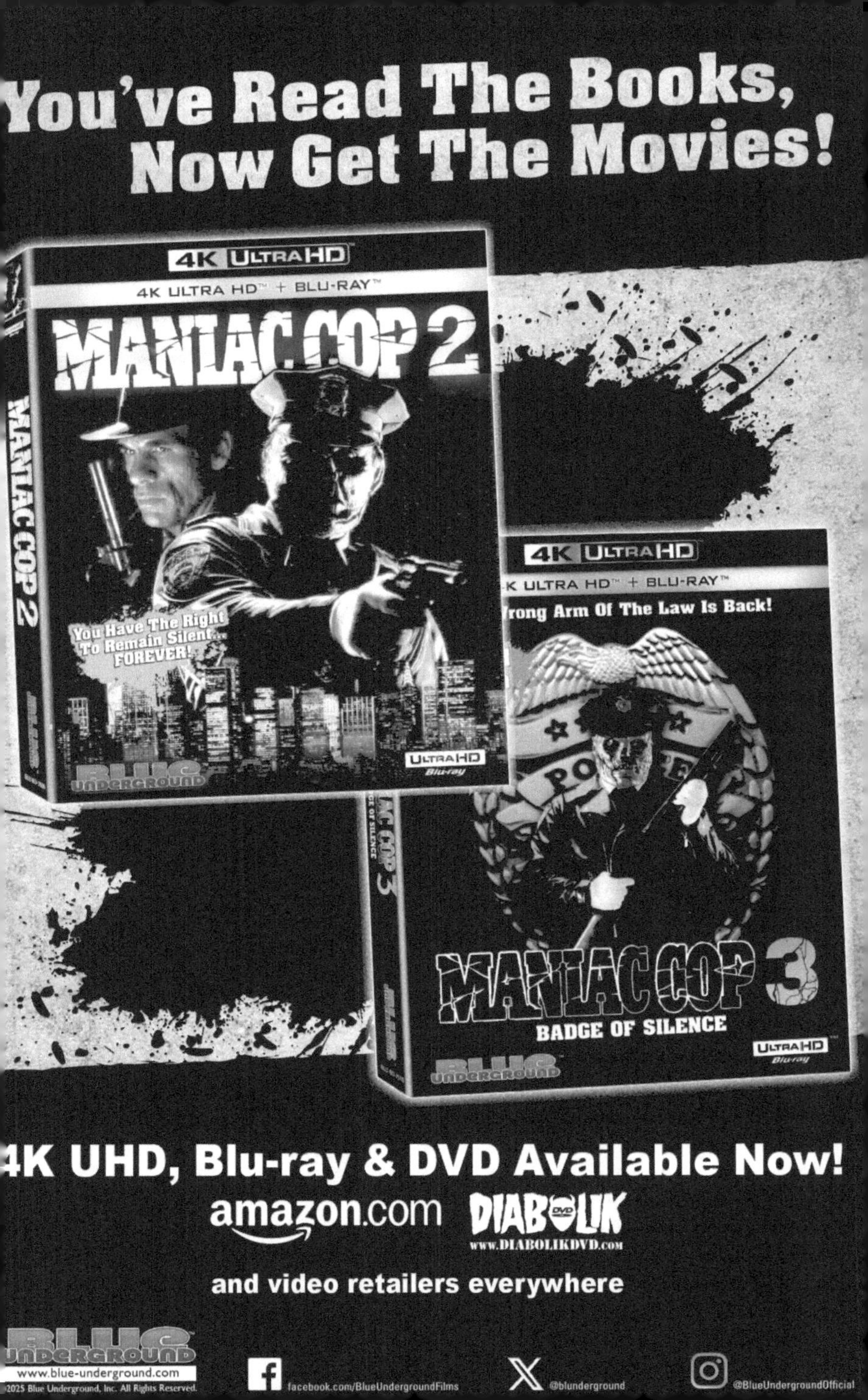

You've Read The Books,
Now Get The Movies!
4K ULTRA HD
4K ULTRA HD™ + BLU-RAY™
MANIAC COP 2
You Have The Right To Remain Silent... FOREVER!
ULTRA HD Blu-ray
BLUE UNDERGROUND
4K ULTRA HD
K ULTRA HD™ + BLU-RAY™
rong Arm Of The Law Is Back!
MANIAC COP 3
BADGE OF SILENCE
ULTRA HD Blu-ray
BLUE UNDERGROUND
4K UHD, Blu-ray & DVD Available Now!
amazon.com
DIABOLIK
WWW.DIABOLIKDVD.COM
and video retailers everywhere
BLUE UNDERGROUND
www.blue-underground.com
©2025 Blue Underground, Inc. All Rights Reserved.
facebook.com/BlueUndergroundFilms
@blunderground
@BlueUndergroundOfficial

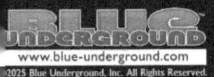

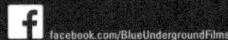

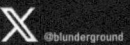

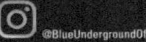

Also by Christian Francis

Official Novelizations

Session 9: The Official Novelization

978-1-916582-59-0 (eBook)

978-1-916582-60-6 (Paperback)

978-1-916582-61-3 (Hardcover)

Released October 2024

★★★★★

"This book was a WILD ride. I was literally biting my nails while getting through it!"

Skylere K (Netgalley)

———

The First Power: The Official Novelization

978-1-916582-95-8 (eBook)

978-1-916582-66-8 (Paperback)

978-1-916582-67-5 (Hardcover)

Released April 2025

Maniac Cop

978-1-916582-68-2 (eBook)

978-1-916582-70-5 (Paperback)

Released May 20 2025

Maniac Cop 2

978-1-916582-71-2 (eBook)

978-1-916582-73-6 (Paperback)

Released May 20 2025

Maniac Cop 3

978-1-916582-74-3 (eBook)

978-1-916582-76-7 (Paperback)

Released May 20 2025

Maniac Cop Trilogy

978-1-916582-69-9 (Hardcover)

978-1-916582-72-9 (Mass Market Paperback)

Released May 20 2025

———

From Echo On Publications

- The Gate (*coming soon*)
- Dee Snider's Strangeland (*coming soon*)
- 3615 Code Père Noël aka Deadly Games (*coming soon*)
- In The Mouth of Madness (*coming soon*)

plus many more to be announced.

From Titan Publishing Group

- The Descent (*coming soon*)

From Encyclopocalypse Publications

- Wishmaster
- Vamp
- Creature, aka Titan Find

Original Novels and Novellas

The Dead Woods

YA Horror

978-1-916582-00-2 (eBook)

978-1-916582-02-6 (Paperback)

978-1-916582-04-0 (Hardcover)

★★★★★

"One of the best YA books I have ever read."

David W Adams (Amazon)

———

The Devil and The Deep

Cosmic Horror

978-1-916582-52-1 (eBook)

978-1-916582-55-2 (Paperback)

978-1-916582-54-5 (Hardcover)

The Sacrifice of Anton Stacey

Horror Novella

978-1-916582-06-4 (eBook)

979-8-386183-59-2 (Paperback)

_____

Everyday Monsters - The Animus Chronicles 1

Dark Fantasy / Horror

978-1-916582-03-3 (eBook)

978-1-916582-09-5 (Paperback)

978-1-916582-10-1 (Hardcover)

_____

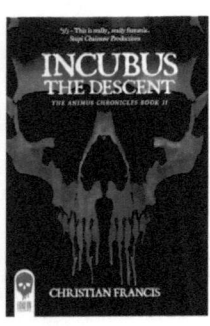

Incubus: The Descent - The Animus Chronicles 2

Dark Fantasy / Horror

978-1-916582-08-8 (eBook)

978-1-916582-11-8 (Paperback)

978-1-916582-12-5 (Hardcover)

Anti Rule: Navigating The Lies About Fiction Writing

Non-Fiction

978-1-916582-01-9 (eBook)

978-1-916582-05-7 (Paperback)

www.ingramcontent.com/pod-product-compliance
Lightning Source LLC
Chambersburg PA
CBHW060547190726
48283CB00003B/903

* 9 7 8 1 9 1 6 5 8 2 7 3 6 *